LANDING
ON
MARVIN GARDENS

LANDING
ON
MARVIN GARDENS

Rona S. Zable

BANTAM BOOKS
NEW YORK · TORONTO · LONDON · SYDNEY · AUCKLAND

To Margie
who never doubted for a minute

LANDING ON MARVIN GARDENS

A Bantam Book / October 1989

Library of Congress Cataloging-in-Publication Data

Zable, Rona S.
   Landing on Marvin Gardens / Rona S. Zable.
      p.   cm.
   Summary: Unable to afford an apartment on their own, fifteen-year-old Katie and her mother reluctantly go to live with stubborn, eccentric Aunt Rose, who turns out to be not just a source of embarrassment but an inspiration as well.
   ISBN 0-553-05839-8
   [1. Aunts—Fiction.   2. Housing—Costs—Fiction.]   I. Title.
PZ7.Z155Lan   1989
[FIC]—dc19
                                                                89-6875
                                                                   CIP
                                                                    AC

Published simultaneously in the United States and Canada

PRINTED IN THE UNITED STATES OF AMERICA

FG   0 9 8 7 6 5 4 3 2 1

62728

LANDING
ON
MARVIN GARDENS

Chapter 1

"Oh, no! Please, Mom—anything but that!"

My mother sighed. "Katie, I've racked my brain. There simply isn't any alternative."

"I'll run away," I cried wildly. "You'll see my picture on a milk carton—and *then* you'll be sorry!"

Another sigh. "I know how you feel. But there's nothing else we can do."

It was a Saturday afternoon in October. Only half an hour earlier, I had written to my dad, telling him how great things had been going for me lately. I was on the staff of the school paper, I had lost four pounds over the summer, and Christopher McConnell had actually said "Hi" to me on the way to study hall.

I was on a *roll*! Until Mom broke the Big News.

"This will push me over the edge," I said. "I'll turn into a street person. You'll see me on *60 Minutes*, living over a grating."

My mother put her arm around me. "It's not forever, Katie. I figure maybe a year or so."

"A *year*? A whole *year*?" I collapsed against the sofa cushions. "I couldn't last there a week—let alone a year."

"Well, I'm afraid you're going to have to," she said briskly, and stood up. "But it might not be that long. Maybe something will break before then."

"Oh, sure," I said. "My heart will break. My sanity threshold will break. You wait and see," I added glumly, "some night you'll come home from the office and you'll find two dead bodies—me and—"

"Shhhhh," Mom whispered. "These walls are paper-thin. She's coming by any minute now. Suppose she hears you?"

"So let her hear me!" My voice rose. "I don't care!"

Just then there was a sharp knock at the door. Mom and I froze.

I pulled myself up from the sofa and went to answer the door. Uh-oh—did she hear me? I wondered. Slowly I unlatched the chain.

My friend Donna stood there grinning at me.

I breathed a sigh of relief. "Oh, it's only you."

"What was all that yelling about?" she asked.

"Come on in," I said. "Have *I* got news for *you*." I steered Donna into my room and shut the door. She sat on the edge of the bed, an expectant look on her face.

"Well," I said, taking a deep breath, "my mother and I have just become two more statistics in the housing crunch. We have to move out of here."

"You have to *move*? How come?"

"Because," I said, "Fairview Dumps—if you can believe it—is going *condo*."

The actual name of our apartment complex is Fairview Downs, but one of the tenants nicknamed it Fairview Dumps since the maintenance is so awful and everything is falling apart.

"Who'd want to buy a condo *here*?" Donna blurted out.

"Not us," I said. "Not even if we could afford it. But there are people who buy condos for investments. They don't live in them, they just rent them out and charge a fortune. My mother says they can get those high rents because there's such a housing shortage around here."

"Oh, wow," Donna said. She thought about the situation for a moment. "Maybe you could get into Willow Terrace. Or that new building downtown."

I shook my head. "Willow Terrace has a two-year waiting list. And Sheffield Towers is a luxury apartment. The rents are out of sight."

"Maybe you could buy a house," Donna said hopefully. For the past couple of years, my mother and I have gone house-hunting on Sundays, but even though she's been scrimping and saving, we still can't afford one.

"It's as if prices of houses go up every day," I said, sighing.

"Couldn't your father help?" Donna suggested. "He sends money, doesn't he?"

"Not very much," I said. "And not regularly—not since he got married again."

Donna's dark eyes were wide with concern. "So what are you going to *do*?"

"Well, we've got our names on the waiting lists for a few middle-income housing developments," I said. "But in the meantime, we are embarking on a new lifestyle. We're the wave of the future. We go where no man has gone before."

"What are you talking about?" Donna asked.

"We are going to *share* a house," I said.

"*Share* a house?" she repeated, puzzled.

And then her eyes nearly popped. "*Oh, no! You wouldn't— you couldn't—you aren't going to live with . . .*"

I nodded. "You got it, Donna. We're going to live with Aunt Rose!"

"Oh, wow—no *wonder* you look so depressed."

I jumped off the bed and started to pace the floor. "Tell me something. You've met my Aunt Rose. What's your honest opinion of her?"

Donna gave the question some consideration. "Well," she said finally, "I would have to say Aunt Rose is nosy, bossy, opinionated, insulting, and old-fashioned."

"Right," I said. "And those are her *good* qualities."

The two of us broke up. "I remember the first time I met her," Donna said, giggling. "I thought she was your grand-mother, not your aunt. It's like she comes from another century."

"Well, she's twenty-five years older than Mom," I said. "She raised my mother after their parents died. And believe me, she'll never let Mom forget it."

There was a soft tap at the door. My mother came in, a worried look on her face. "Katie, when Aunt Rose stops by she's going to ask what things we want to take with us. Please—be nice. You know she really *means* well."

"Oh, sure," I said. "Like Attila the Hun—he really meant well, too."

I didn't mean to be tough on Mom. I knew she had a lot on her mind, between work and moving, not to mention the prospect of living with Aunt Rose.

"Aunt Rose runs a tight ship," Mom admitted.

At that very moment, there was a horrendous pounding at the door.

"Speaking of tight ships," I whispered, "that sounds like the *Titanic* herself!"

The three of us scrambled out into the living room. By now the pounding on the door had grown louder.

"*Are you all deaf in there?*" Aunt Rose's shrill voice called out from the hallway. Doors started opening down the hall, and we knew the neighbors were listening, wondering what was going on.

I was laughing so hard I could barely unlatch the chain. All the while Aunt Rose kept yelling things like "*Don't you even know how to open your own door?*"

Finally the door swung open, and in marched Aunt Rose. Her dyed-black hair, freshly waved and teased from her weekly Saturday-morning hairdresser appointment, was lacquered into submission. Under her black raincoat she wore a black-and-white-striped dress with pleats so sharp it looked as if they could stab you.

4

Her narrow black eyes squinted behind big harlequin glasses as she took in everything . . . our worn-out furniture, the dust on the coffee table, Donna's jacket carelessly tossed on the sofa.

Aunt Rose didn't bother saying hello. "Hoo, your neighbor downstairs, what kind of *food* does she cook? It smells like she's boiling rubber bands! Or maybe," my aunt added darkly, "it's true what they say—maybe she's cooking a *cat!*"

Mom started to laugh. "Oh, Rose, it's just that Viji uses different spices than we do. And she'd certainly *never* cook a cat—she's a vegetarian."

"I don't care what country she's from," Aunt Rose said, not even listening, "all I know is, a person could choke from that smell."

Mom quickly steered my aunt to the kitchen. We could hear her snapping open cabinets and shutting them smartly. "The coffee maker I could use," Aunt Rose said in her loud voice. "And you may as well bring the microwave. Hmph—not a pot to put flowers in, Marilyn, but you can afford a microwave."

Donna and I went back to my room. We were planning to go to the early show at the mall cinema. My mother was supposed to drive us there, and Donna's parents were going to pick us up at nine-thirty when the mall closes.

Donna collapsed on my bed, laughing. "Your aunt is too much. She's not to be believed."

"What don't you believe?" Aunt Rose trumpeted as she barged into my bedroom.

My heart sank. I was getting a preview of what it would be like to live with Aunt Rose. I wondered if I could put a lock on the door of my room.

"I told your mother to bring the color TV," Aunt Rose said. "We can put it in the den. What do you need to bring with you?"

I looked around the room. "Okay, let me see. Well, my reading lamp, my typewriter, my yellow comforter . . ."

Aunt Rose wasn't paying attention. She was inspecting the clutter in my bedroom.

"You know," she said, "it'll be good for you to live in my house, Katie. Maybe you'll learn to be a little neat."

"Although," she added, "it didn't help your mother." She turned to Donna and confided, "Marilyn isn't neat either. Did you know I brought Marilyn up? She's my baby sister. Henry and I took her in even though we already had a child of our own, my Sylvia . . . " Aunt Rose went on, lost in recollection. "But did *I* complain? Oh, no—not me."

Donna was a brand-new audience, and Aunt Rose went through the whole story. I just stood behind my aunt, rolling my eyes, and Donna tried to keep a straight face.

". . . And then I said to my Henry, 'So what if it means another mouth to feed. I'm used to making sacrifices . . .' "

"Rose," Mom said as she came into my room, "the girls have to leave soon. I'm driving them to the movies."

Aunt Rose raised penciled black eyebrows. "A Saturday night and no dates? How come they don't have dates?"

"It's different nowadays," Mom explained. "They don't really go out on dates. And besides, Katie and Donna are only fifteen."

"Hah," Aunt Rose snorted, "when *I* was fifteen, I had plenty of dates, plenty of boyfriends."

In your dreams, Aunt Rose, I said under my breath. It so happens I know Aunt Rose was *never* fifteen. She was *born* old!

"Nosiree," she continued with relish, "you'd never catch *me* sitting home with my girlfriends on a Saturday night. I had plenty to do—boyfriends, parties, dances—you name it."

"Oh, well, *that* should certainly make the girls feel a lot better," Mom said dryly. Aunt Rose wasn't listening. She had walked over to the mirror where Donna was fixing her hair.

"It's not like you're that bad looking," Aunt Rose said. "You're no American beauties, but I've seen homelier girls get dates."

6

Mom pulled at her arm. "Rose, really—it's getting late and the girls will miss the movie."

Aunt Rose didn't budge. She stood there, fascinated, watching as Donna put the finishing touches to her hair.

In what sounded like a tone of admiration, Aunt Rose said, "My, my—look at that. The hairstyles you girls have these days—they're so—so *ugly*."

The room was silent except for the thump of Donna's hairbrush hitting the floor. I bit my tongue. Mom rolled her eyes to the ceiling and sighed.

"Well," said Aunt Rose, glancing at her watch, "I better get a move on, too. My widows' Grief Group is having a potluck supper tonight."

Then Aunt Rose started to ramble on about Uncle Henry and how "destroyed" she was when he passed away seven years ago. She's been carrying on like that for years, and I'm sure she really does miss him a lot. But the truth is, Aunt Rose is the merriest widow in America. She's never *been* so happy since she joined that Grief Group. She plays bridge, has potluck suppers, goes on trips, and talks about grief with her lady friends.

I raced to the closet to get her raincoat. "You better hurry," I told her. "You'll be late and everybody will eat up all the good things."

"You said a mouthful," Aunt Rose agreed. "They're like vultures, the way they grab that food. You'd think it was going out of style."

We heaved a collective sigh of relief when she finally drove off in her old Buick.

Donna looked dazed. "I've never *met* anyone like your aunt before."

"And you only saw her in action for twenty minutes," I said. "Can you picture what it's going to be like *living* with her?"

Mom fished the car keys out of her pocketbook. "Now,

Katie, we have to be grateful. Rose is offering us a place to live." She gave me a long, steady look. "A studio apartment at Sheffield Towers would take three weeks' pay. Three weeks to pay the rent—and there isn't even a bedroom. It's as simple as that."

Mom was right. There wasn't a better alternative. I knew I had to stop complaining and make the best of it.

None of us said much on the way to the mall. Mom dropped us off at Cinema World where we saw a comedy, but I couldn't concentrate on the movie. All I could think about was life with Aunt Rose.

The more I thought about it, the more depressed I felt. I was convinced that all the good things that had been happening lately would change. My creative juices would dry up, and I wouldn't be able to write and they'd kick me off the school paper. I would probably gain back those four pounds and more. I was already on my way. Without even realizing it, I had finished off the Big Buy Buttered Popcorn and was absently tearing open a package of Reese's Pieces.

And as for Christopher McConnell—even if by some miracle he ever *did* get interested in me, I'm sure Aunt Rose would somehow manage to ruin everything.

A year or so, Mom had said. I popped another handful of Reese's Pieces into my mouth. Who cared about the calories? I needed the energy.

I had a hunch this was going to be the wackiest year of my whole life!

Chapter 2

We moved out of our apartment the last weekend of October. Mom had put most of our furniture in storage, and on Saturday morning we packed up the rest of our things in the car and headed to Aunt Rose's house on the other side of town.

"Good-bye, Fairview Downs," Mom said as we drove out of the parking lot. "And hello, one sixty-six Hemlock Street."

I sat up with a jolt.

"Uh-oh," I said. "I sure hope that's not an omen—Hemlock, I mean."

"What are you talking about?" Mom asked.

"Hemlock," I said, "was the name of the poison they made Socrates drink."

She started to laugh. "Leave it to you to think of something like that. But you shouldn't be so negative, Katie," she added. "You have to be *positive*."

"I'm positive, all right. Positive I'll hate living there."

That was Mom's cue to launch into one of the many rah-rah pep talks she had been giving me for the past few weeks, namely on how Life Can Be Beautiful With Aunt Rose.

They included such positive thoughts as: "It's going to be so nice living in a real house with a yard instead of a cramped little apartment."

And: "Aunt Rose has a washing machine and a dryer so we won't have to lug our clothes to the Laundromat."

And: "It'll be nice for you to have someone in the house when you get home from school."

"You should have quit while you were ahead with the washer and dryer," I told my mother. "Aunt Rose is not exactly what you'd want to come home to."

We turned the corner onto Hemlock Street, which is one of the older residential sections of Pennington. My heart sank as I looked at Aunt Rose's big, ugly, gray-shingled house.

When I was a little kid, I really believed her house was haunted. It's dark and gloomy, set back from the other houses on the street, and everything inside seems dark, too. There are heavy drapes over the room-darkening shades to make sure not a ray of sun gets in and fades the mahogany furniture. There are lace doilies on the dark maroon sofa and chairs, and everywhere you look little ceramic and glass knickknacks sit just waiting to be broken.

Mom pulled up in front of the house, and we started unloading some heavy cartons from the trunk.

A thought suddenly occurred to me as we trudged up the front steps. "Mom, do you realize in two days it'll be Halloween?"

At that moment Aunt Rose opened the front door. "Don't mark up the walls with those boxes," she warned.

"Talk about trick or treat," I said resignedly.

Actually, my aunt was in a wonderful mood. "This is just like old times," she told Mom happily. "It reminds me of when you came to live with us, Marilyn. Do you remember?"

She led the way upstairs to the bedrooms. As always, the house smelled of pine-scented disinfectant. Aunt Rose has dedicated her life to ridding the world of dust and dirt; Mom and I, on the other hand, can coexist quite nicely with the stuff.

"Marilyn, you're going to have your old room back again. And Kate can have Sylvia's room," Aunt Rose announced.

A more appropriate name would be "Sylvia's Shrine." My

aunt carries on as if her daughter's old room is some kind of designated historic site. She keeps it just the way it was when Cousin Sylvia left, before she went off to college in Oregon and stayed there to get married.

I never got to know my cousin since there was such a big age difference between us, but I've been hearing the Saga of Sylvia for years from Aunt Rose. Apparently my cousin is close to perfection in every way except for the fact that she lives on the West Coast and she's now divorced. Sylvia has two bratty kids and the few times she's visited here, I've gotten stuck with taking care of them.

I set my cartons of books down on the floor and looked around. I hadn't been in Sylvia's room for years, so I'd forgotten what it looked like.

It was not what you would call a warm and cozy place. The walls were stark white. The bed had a snow-white chenille spread. The lace doilies on the dresser and night table were Clorox-white. The window shades were white. The ruffled curtains were white.

"Oh, wow," I said, pretending to shield my eyes, "I could get snow blindness here!"

Aunt Rose took that as a compliment. "I like a white bedroom, too," she agreed.

Like a Marine drill sergeant, she marched us down the hall to Mom's old room, all the while talking about the day years back when my mother had come to live with them.

"It seems like only yesterday," Aunt Rose recalled. "You were just a teeny, tiny tot, Marilyn."

"Rose, I was eleven years old," Mom reminded her.

We went back out to the car to get another load of things. "Mom," I whispered, "that _room_—it's so _white_! I'll have to wear sunglasses to study."

"Don't worry," she said. "When you put your yellow comforter on the bed and something colorful on the walls, it'll look nice."

"And how about your room," I said. "You got the Presidential Suite."

That made Mom laugh. When Aunt Rose had the upstairs painted a few years back, she got a sudden burst of patriotism. She hung pictures of presidents on the walls: George Washington, Abraham Lincoln as a young man, a print of Teddy Roosevelt about to lead a charge, plus a framed snapshot of Aunt Rose and Uncle Henry standing in front of Mount Vernon when they took a bus tour of Washington, D.C., and Virginia.

We found out later that Aunt Rose bought the president prints dirt cheap at a garage sale.

"I hate that picture of George Washington," Mom said, shuddering. "His eyes always seem to be staring at you."

"I know what you mean," I said. "It's going to feel weird having the father of our country watch you undress."

Mom and I made a few more trips, bringing things into the house while Aunt Rose supervised. I went back to the car for the last load of clothes.

As I was locking the car door, a voice said, "Need any help?"

I looked up over a tangle of wire hangers. *Was I seeing things?*

There—in gray sweat pants—wearing the crimson and gold Pennington High football jacket, stood Christopher McConnell.

I couldn't help it. The clothes slid off my arm and dropped to the sidewalk. Chris bent down to pick them up.

Of all the rotten, miserable times for a guy to see me, this had to be the worst. I hadn't bothered to put on makeup or fix my hair, and I had to have been wearing the world's oldest jeans and my mother's ugliest sweater.

"Uh—that's all right," I croaked. "Just—uh—throw everything right on top."

There is something mortifying about having a guy you

hardly know help carry your clothes, especially things like a ratty bathrobe.

"It's no trouble." Chris strode up the front steps, still carrying my clothes.

The front door flew open. "Give me those!" Aunt Rose ordered. She grabbed the clothes from Chris as if he were about to steal my stunning wardrobe.

"You're welcome, Mrs. Cronin," Chris said very pointedly.

"Uh, thanks," I managed to call out just before my aunt slammed the door in his face.

I felt totally humiliated. "Well, don't just *stand* there with your mouth open," she said. "Let's go hang up these clothes before they get even *more* wrinkled."

I scrambled up the stairs after her. "Aunt Rose," I said, "that boy who helped me—do you know him?"

"Well, most naturally I know him. He's one of the McConnells. He used to be our paperboy."

"Really?" I tried to sound nonchalant. "Does he live around here?"

"He lives on the next street in the yellow house. That place needs a paint job, believe you me." Aunt Rose was busily straightening out my hangers, making sure they all faced the same way.

She kept talking as she moved my clothes around in the closet, telling me stories about her neighbors, and I understood then why Uncle Henry used to call her "the eyes and ears of the world." She knew everyone's business!

But I was so excited to learn that Chris lived nearby that I even gave Aunt Rose a hug when she finished straightening my closet.

"That looks terrific," I said. "How come *I* can't make my closet look that good?"

"Because," said Aunt Rose, "you're a slob."

She sounded quite pleased about it.

*   *   *

Mom fixed dinner that night, thank goodness, because my aunt Rose is a terrible cook. I've got a theory that people who are very neat and organized usually can't cook, and people who aren't good at housekeeping can make anything taste great. Even Aunt Rose loved my mother's honey-glazed chicken.

The rest of the evening was dreary. A heavy rain started up, slamming against the windowpanes. Aunt Rose went off to play bridge with her Grief Group. Mom and I watched TV in the den. There was an old movie she wanted to watch about an Egyptian mummy with a curse on the tomb.

I knew I shouldn't stay up to watch it—horror movies really scare me—but like a fool, I did.

I couldn't fall asleep that night. Everything in Aunt Rose's house seemed so strange. My room was too white. My mattress was too hard. Back in our old apartment, Mom's bedroom had been right next to mine, but now, her room was down a long, dark hallway.

The weather didn't help either. Outside my window, the branches of a tree kept bending in the howling wind, making weird shadows against the white curtains.

Finally I fell into a fitful sleep. Then suddenly, around two o'clock in the morning, I woke up. I had been having a scary dream about Halloween and a mummy's curse.

I clutched my yellow comforter around me and turned over.

Then I heard the noise downstairs.

I held my breath. Again I heard the noise. It was a strange, scuffing sound. As if somebody—or something—was dragging slowly up the stairs.

Scuff-clump. Scuff-clump.

Up the stairs it came. *Scuff-clump.*

Louder! Closer!

Terror pounded in my throat. My bedroom door was half-closed, so there was no way I could see whatever was out there in the hallway. I sat upright, rigid against the headboard of the bed.

Then the door of my bedroom slowly opened.

It was like a scene out of a Stephen King novel. The rain pounding on the windows, the wind moaning and shrieking outside.

And as the doorknob turned, a ghostly apparition floated into my room!

I stared in horror at the creature. Streams of gauzy white had been wound around its head.

Like an Egyptian mummy!

"What-do-you-want?" I whispered, my teeth chattering.

The pale figure kept coming closer. Gibberish came from its mouth. "Ronnercrozyerinner."

"DON'T YOU COME NEAR ME!" I yelled.

The creature kept coming toward me. "Wusronwitcher. Eyeonyronnercrozyerinner. . . ."

I leaped out of bed, cowering in the corner. "GO AWAY!" I kept screaming and screaming at the top of my lungs. "SOMEBODY—HELP ME!"

Chapter 3

"Oh, wow!" Donna kept saying over and over. "Oh, wow!"

We were sprawled out on the twin beds in her pink and green bedroom. I had rushed over to Donna's house after lunch on Sunday to tell her all the details.

"So then," I continued, "Mom came running into the room, hollering like a crazy woman."

"Oh, wow, what did your aunt Rose do?"

I buried my face in the pillow as I recalled the events of last night. "It was awful. I was hysterical, Mom was hysterical, and that made Aunt Rose hysterical. We were all screaming and then the telephone rang. The people next door heard all the noise and they wanted to know if they should call the police."

"What *I* don't understand," Donna said, shaking her head, "is why your aunt was talking so *funny*."

"Because," I groaned, "Aunt Rose had her *teeth* out. I never even knew she *had* false teeth."

Donna kept filing her nails, trying not to laugh. "What was she doing in your room anyhow?"

"She wanted to make sure my window was closed. It was raining like crazy during the night. And you know how Aunt Rose is."

"She must have looked like something out of the Twilight Zone," Donna said.

"How was *I* supposed to know what she puts on her head at night? She looked like an Egyptian mummy to *me*."

"What was it?" Donna asked.

"Toilet paper," I said. I felt my face turn red as I recalled the incident. "Aunt Rose wraps toilet paper around her head to keep her hairdo in. Did you ever hear such a crazy thing?"

"As a matter of fact, yes," Donna said, putting down her emery board. "My grandmother does that sometimes."

"I didn't know that," I said, feeling completely stupid. "I mean, I never saw Aunt Rose that way—with her teeth out and her head all wrapped up in half a roll of toilet paper, and those big, floppy slippers on her feet. I guess I've led a sheltered life."

This time Donna couldn't smother her giggles. The two of us had a good laugh. "You poor thing," Donna said when we caught our breath. "What a way to spend your first night there. I bet your aunt was mad."

"Well, that's the funny thing. After Aunt Rose calmed down, she wasn't that upset. She thought I was flaky—but then, she *always* did."

I wondered if I might have hurt Aunt Rose's feelings the way I carried on at the sight of her. I had to admit she handled it pretty well.

"Anyhow," I added, "it gives her something to talk about with her Grief Girls."

"Her *what*?"

"You know—the widows' Grief Group she belongs to. My aunt is the only person I know who makes a hobby out of grief. Anyhow, this morning, she was on the phone calling up all the Griefees and telling them how her crazy niece thought she was a mummy. It gave them all a good laugh."

Donna carefully applied base coat to her long nails, not missing a word of our conversation. "Well, one thing you can say about living with Aunt Rose—it's one surprise after another."

"Surprise I can take," I said. "It's *shock* I'm worried about. Oh, that reminds me, I forgot to tell you about Chris McConnell. Would you believe he walked by yesterday while I was carrying my stuff into the house?"

I proceeded to tell Donna how Aunt Rose had slammed the door in his face, and Donna kept up a sympathetic chorus of oh-wow's while she finished her manicure.

"Anyhow," I concluded with a sigh, "even if by some miracle Chris ever noticed me—or if by some miracle I ever got a boyfriend of any kind—I know Aunt Rose would manage to ruin everything."

"I wish *I* had a boyfriend," Donna said dreamily. That was our favorite topic of conversation lately. "I mean, I wish we *both* had boyfriends."

"Me, too."

Donna held up one hand so I could admire her French manicure. "Well, Katie, you *could* have a boyfriend if you wanted. I think Mike Matthews kind of likes you."

"*Mike Matthews?*" I repeated. "Get real, Donna. He likes me about as much as I like him. He's a first-class conceited jerk!"

"Mike is a nice guy," she protested. "There's something kind of appealing about him, even though he's a brain."

"Mike Matthews is about as appealing as earwax," I said. "Don't forget, I've known him since fourth grade. He was a pill even back then."

What I didn't want to admit was that I was jealous of Mike Matthews.

Ever since we were nine years old, we'd been school rivals. One year I would be the top student; the next year it would be Mike.

But lately my grades had taken a nosedive. Maybe I was

burned out or tired of being a grind. I just didn't feel like hitting the books. Mike, of course, just kept on getting A's while I trailed behind.

He had always been a whiz in subjects like math and science, which happen to be my weak spots. But what *bothers* me is that Mike also gets straight A's in English and social science, which are my strong points!

"There's something cute about him," Donna persisted. "The way he teases you, I really think he likes you."

I changed the subject. Mike was certainly not my favorite topic. When Donna's nails were dry, we went downstairs to the kitchen and ate a few of her mother's caramel brownies while we quizzed each other on French vocabulary. After that, Donna walked me halfway back to Aunt Rose's house.

I took the scenic route the rest of the way—namely, past Chris McConnell's house. It was easy enough to spot—a tiny yellow house with paint peeling just like Aunt Rose had said.

When I got to the back door, I realized I'd forgotten my key. Aunt Rose opened the door for me. "You'd forget your head if it wasn't stuck to your shoulders," she said, but she didn't seem upset. "Two ladies from the Grief Group want to meet you."

Before I could protest, she had dragged me over to the dining room table where two women sat drinking coffee and eating big slabs of what I knew was Sara Lee pound cake.

My aunt likes everyone to think she does her own baking, but she really buys pastry, hides the boxes, and never ever admits it's not homemade. That very morning I had spotted the Sara Lee cake defrosting on the kitchen counter. I knew for sure there was a Sara Lee box neatly flattened in the trash can.

"This is Katie, my niece," Aunt Rose called out gaily. "The crazy one I told you about—that thought I was a ghost. It's a wonder I didn't have a coronary. And these"—she pointed to the two women—"are Mrs. Grimes and Mrs. Utley."

"Every time somebody says 'coronary,' I think of my poor

Fred." Mrs. Utley dabbed at her eyes with a napkin. Then she cut herself another huge slice of cake.

"Delicious, Rose," she pronounced. "I must have your recipe."

Little Mrs. Grimes was smiling up at me. "My, you're a pretty girl, Katie. What beautiful hair you have. Is it naturally curly?"

"Yes, it is, thanks," I said.

"Oh, and the cute little figures on girls these days." Mrs. Utley gave a huge sigh, popping big slivers of cake into her birdlike mouth. "And the clothes they wear—you have to be so *slim* to wear things like that."

Mrs. Grimes nodded. "The fashion designers only think of teenagers," she said ruefully. "The clothes they're showing this season—well, all *I* can say is, the world of fashion will have to go along without *me!*"

"It always *has*, Edith," Aunt Rose snorted. "It always has."

On Monday morning when I straggled downstairs to the kitchen for breakfast, there was Aunt Rose all girdled and dressed.

She's hard to take on an empty stomach.

"Is that what you let your daughter wear to school, Marilyn?" she demanded. "She'll freeze her you-know-what off!"

No sooner had Mom reassured her that I hardly ever catch cold, Aunt Rose pounced again. "Is that all she eats for breakfast? She'll get anemic."

She nagged Mom, too. "Look at the suit your mother's wearing," Aunt Rose clucked, eyeing Mom's bargain basement outfit. "They'll think *she's* the lawyer, not the secretary! Tell your mother not to dress so fancy or they'll figure they're paying her too much."

Mom is a legal secretary for a big law firm, though I think she's smart enough to be a lawyer or at least a paralegal. I don't know why she doesn't go to night school for paralegal training, but I wonder if it's because she doesn't want to leave me alone too much. I think sometimes she feels that she has to make up for being a single parent by spending twice as much time with me.

Mom was her usual cheerful self, despite Aunt Rose's relentless nag-a-thon. All in all, it was not the most pleasant way to start the day.

It was the very first time I had ever walked to high school. When we lived at Fairview Dumps, I had to take the bus because the apartments were on the outskirts of town.

I wanted to walk with Donna, but this morning I had to leave a few minutes earlier to go to the Student Affairs office to change my address.

"One sixty-six Hemlock Street," the secretary repeated after I'd given her the information. "In care of Rose Cronin. I went to school with a Sylvia Cronin. Any relation?"

"That's Sylvia's mother," I said. "Sylvia's my cousin."

"Oh, Mrs. *Cronin*. Boy, do I remember her. She used to come in practically every day—bringing Sylvia's lunch or her violin. She even used to call the office and leave messages for Sylvia reminding her if she had to baby-sit or do something after school."

"Wow, poor Sylvia," I said. "The way Aunt Rose talks, you'd think Sylvia was perfect. I'm kind of glad to hear she's not."

"I just hope for your sake that Mrs. Cronin isn't as obsessed with you as she was with her daughter. So what's Sylvia up to these days, anyway?"

"She lives out in Oregon with her twin sons."

"Oregon," the woman said, shaking her head. "Sylvia must've had enough of her mother's nagging to move that far away."

Guess so, I thought to myself. The bell for first period

rang, and I hurried off to English class, breathless as I slid into my seat.

Mike Matthews, who sits across from me, leaned over and whispered, "I hear you moved. I knew you couldn't stay away from me. You know, of course, I live a couple of streets down from Hemlock."

Donna must have told Mike I was now in his neighborhood.

"Oh, joy," I said. "My cup runneth over."

Mrs. Wetzel banged on her desk to shush us. "Quiet, please. I have an announcement to make."

I was hardly listening. For some reason, the thought had just hit me that we might still be living with Aunt Rose next summer, and that sure got me depressed. I wondered if my dad would let me visit him in Atlanta for the summer. Or maybe my grandparents would invite me to Florida.

". . . I'm sure all of you are familiar with the Jonathan Waring awards and scholarships for juniors and seniors," Mrs. Wetzel was saying. "This year, for the first time, there will be an event for sophomores—the first annual Jonathan Waring Essay Competition."

My ears perked up. For as long as I could remember, I had always gotten A's on compositions and writing projects. In fact, my first assignment for the school paper was to write an essay on cheating.

"This is a *very* prestigious award," Mrs. Wetzel went on, her cheeks pink with excitement. "As you know, Jonathan Waring is a philanthropist who has endowed many institutions in Pennington."

We all knew about Jonathan Waring. There was a street named after him, a grammar school, a brand-new wing at the hospital.

As she droned on, I got more excited. The first prize was a $500 bond plus a write-up in the local newspaper. And, she reminded us, winning the competition would certainly be an advantage when it came to applying for one of the Waring scholarships during senior year.

Mrs. Wetzel adjusted her glasses and read from the green school bulletin. "The essay competition will be held on a Saturday morning in February, the exact date to be announced. Two factors will determine the winning essay—the student's grade-point average as well as the content and caliber of the writing."

As Mrs. Wetzel spoke, I had this fantasy of me up there on the podium, receiving first prize for my essay . . . and Chris McConnell out in the audience, suddenly noticing me—*really* noticing me—for the first time. . . .

"The top ten students in the sophomore class have been chosen to compete," Mrs. Wetzel continued. My heart started to pound. *Was I in that top ten?* Lately my grades hadn't been so hot. I had been goofing off. Maybe I wouldn't even be able to compete! I sat rigidly in my seat, hanging on her every word.

"Three students from Mr. Siegal's class, three from Mrs. Boyle's class, two from Miss Perrin's class, and"—she broke into a big smile—"two students from this class." God, she was certainly prolonging the suspense!

"The two from this class are Michael Matthews and Kate Williams." Mrs. Wetzel was positively beaming. "I anticipate that the first prize winner will be either Kate or Michael."

There was a scattered round of applause, which was started by Mike himself. Somehow Mike can get away with stuff like that without being considered a conceited show-off—everyone just thinks he's great.

Mike raised his hand. "Does it say what the essay is supposed to be about?"

Mrs. Wetzel consulted her bulletin. "It says the topic will be announced that day. However," she said, "if I were to hazard a guess, knowing Jonathan Waring's background, I'd say

24

the topic would probably have to do with some current social issue."

The rest of the period was a blur. Mrs. Wetzel droned on about topics and the art of the essay and how we had to keep our "creative juices flowing."

There were a lot of social issues I could get fired up about. In fact, I've already written letters to the editor about certain issues and the *Pennington Daily Dispatch* has published two of them. Aunt Rose calls me the attorney general.

When the bell rang, Mike stood up and grabbed my arm. "Hey, Katie—it's like old times. You and me—we're at it again."

I shook off his hand. "Correction, it's you and me and eight others."

"Oh, they're just for show." Mike grinned cheerfully. "They won't make it. I know who some of them are—Melissa Cohen, Wayne Erlich, Janine what's-her-name, Don Leung, and that foreign exchange student. The thing is, they've got good marks, but none of them are particularly good writers."

And neither are you, Mike Matthews, I wanted to say, but I clamped my mouth shut.

"And neither am I," Mike said, echoing my thoughts. "But I've got a high grade average. *You* can really knock off the essay part, though. You'll have the judges crying in their tally sheets or whatever they use."

"Listen, Mike," I said through clenched teeth. "The fact is, even if I wrote the most fantastic essay anyone could write, it won't necessarily mean that much. Not if someone's got a higher grade-point average."

"Well, Katie," Mike said, "your grades could be right up there, too."

We both knew what he meant. At the end of last year Mike had told me I was lazy about my grades. "You ought to be getting A's," he had said to me then. "But you figure because you're a good writer and it comes easy, you don't have to bother with English or lit. And you bluff your way through social studies. You could do a lot better grade-wise and you know it."

I knew Mike was right, but I was hurt. "Well," I had snapped, "we can't *all* be grinds."

Mike had hardly spoken to me for the next couple of weeks. Not even to tease me.

So here we were once again, competing against each other. Out in the hall, Donna rushed over to me. "Katie," she cried, "you'll win that prize for sure."

As the two of us headed to our next class, Chris McConnell passed by. He didn't even see me, he was so busy talking with a pretty little blonde. I recognized her as one of the new cheerleaders. Chris was so tall he had to bend down to hear what she was saying.

We had a substitute in geometry class, so I didn't have to pay much attention. The poor woman was just trying to keep us reasonably quiet and kill time till Miss Murdock came back.

All I could think about was the essay competition. *I really need to win*, I told myself. *I need some kind of victory to cheer me up and make this year bearable.*

I opened up my notebook and started to write:

Goal #1—Pull up grades
Goal #2—Win J.W. essay contest
Goal #3—Get C. to ask me out

But it wasn't going to be easy accomplishing these goals—especially living with Aunt Rose. How could I study in that snow-white bedroom? And Aunt Rose *hates* rock music—how could I work without my stereo? Where else could I do homework—in Mom's bedroom with George Washington smirking as I struggled with geometry?

As for Chris McConnell, I had this vision of him ringing the doorbell on our first date—and Aunt Rose opening the door and yelling at him for giving her the wrong change when he was the paperboy.

But the toughest goal of all would be to write the winning essay. How was I going to keep my creative juices from drying up?

Living with Aunt Rose was going to take more creativity than winning any contest!

Chapter 4

After school, I invited Donna to come over to our house because I didn't want to face Aunt Rose all by myself. As I unlocked the back door, I could hear voices in the living room. I figured some of the Grief Girls were visiting.

Donna and I were putting our books down on the kitchen table when suddenly Aunt Rose yelled out, "WATCH IT— THERE'S SOMEONE BEHIND YOU!"

Donna and I froze in terror. I could feel my insides turning to ice water.

After what seemed like an eternity, there was a burst of music and then some more voices talking and laughing.

"OH, DON'T LISTEN TO HER!" Aunt Rose cried out in agitation. "SHE'S A TROUBLEMAKER."

Another burst of music. Donna and I shuddered in relief. "Your aunt sure gets into those soap operas, doesn't she?" Donna said, her voice shaky.

Donna and I tiptoed down the hallway and peeked into the living room. As usual, the curtains and shades were drawn. Aunt Rose was sitting on the edge of a hard-backed maroon chair, twisting a handkerchief as she watched a soap opera on her vintage black-and-white Magnavox console.

No, let me correct part of that statement. Other people *watch* television. Aunt Rose *lives* it.

29

"Don't be such a fool! You never learn! He's cheating on you."

"Look at that," I whispered to Donna. "She even nags the actors!"

We tiptoed back to the kitchen. A few seconds later, Aunt Rose joined us.

"Oh, I didn't even hear you come in," she said, sitting down at the table. "I was watching my stories. You won't believe what's going on. Hoo, that mother-in-law is some troublemaker, I tell you. I've got *her* number."

"Donna and I have to do some studying," I started to say, but I wasn't fast enough to stop Aunt Rose from launching into the endless plot of her favorite soap opera. Donna's eyes glazed over.

Luckily, Mom came home from the office early, so Aunt Rose never did finish the end of her story. She was so happy to have a new captive audience, she even invited Donna to stay for dinner.

Donna thanked Aunt Rose profusely but explained that she had to get home to help her mother since it was Halloween and they always had lots of trick-or-treaters.

We had an early dinner so we would be finished by the time the kids started ringing our bell.

My mother announced she was going out to a meeting at the library. "They're starting up a Coalition for Affordable Housing," she explained. "It's something I'd like to get involved in."

"That's great, Mom." I was surprised. My mother hardly ever used to go out at night when we lived at Fairview Dumps. Maybe now that we were living in a safer neighborhood she felt better about it.

"Maybe you'll *meet* someone there," Aunt Rose said pointedly. "Someone who'll take care of *you* for a change." She was referring to the fact that Mom helped put my father through college and supported him while he bounced from one job to another. As usual my mother ignored the comments.

I took another helping of baked beef stew, one of my favorite meals. I like it better than steak.

"Oh, Katie, I forgot to tell you," Mom said. "I stopped off at the library on my way home to check the time of the meeting tonight, and guess who I saw there—Cindy Harrington from Fairview Downs."

"Cindy? I haven't seen her since they moved. What'd she have to say?"

"That's the funny thing—it seemed like she was trying to avoid me." My mother set her fork down and added thoughtfully, "I almost didn't recognize her. She looked . . . awful."

Cindy Harrington looked awful? That was hard to believe. Cindy, who had long honey-blond hair and big blue eyes, was one of the prettiest girls I knew. Cindy had lived down the hall from us at Fairview Downs until she and her family moved to a duplex on the other side of town. I hadn't seen her since they left, which was about six months before we did.

I liked Cindy, but we didn't really travel in the same circles since she went to Bishop Reardon, the Catholic high school. But we used to walk to the bus stop together, and we always had nice long talks. Occasionally when my mother had to work late or went out for the evening, I'd go over to Cindy's apartment. I liked her family. She had a younger brother and sister, and her mother worked in a nursing home. Cindy's father had died of a brain tumor before they moved to Fairview Downs.

"Less talk now and more action," Aunt Rose ordered. "The kids will be coming by for trick or treat before you know it."

We finished dinner and cleared the table. Mom went upstairs to get ready for her meeting. Aunt Rose said she would rinse the dishes because I never get all the food off.

She put me in charge of the candy tray, but as it turned out, she did not particularly care for the way I arrange candy.

"The Tootsie Rolls should go over there"—she pointed—"and the Milky Ways over here."

"What's the difference?" I asked.

"What's the *difference*?" Aunt Rose had to think about that a moment. "Because it doesn't look right, that's why."

"It looks okay to me."

"Oh, *you*. What do *you* know? You're not organized."

I had to laugh. Sometimes Aunt Rose was more rigid than her girdle. "I promise you," I joked, "the sun will still rise tomorrow and the tides will go in and out—even if the Tootsie Rolls are on that side of the tray."

"Sylvia used to arrange the candy so nice," Aunt Rose countered. Then she launched into yet another Sylvia story—this one about how wonderfully Sylvia could knit and sew.

One more story about Superwoman Sylvia and I was going to barf!

Mom left for her meeting. I decided to do my homework on the kitchen table so I would be downstairs when the kids came for trick or treat. I could hear them going up and down the block, ringing doorbells and chorusing thank-you's to the neighbors.

But nobody rang our bell.

"The kids don't come around much on Halloween anymore," Aunt Rose complained. "I wonder why not."

I found out why not a few minutes later. The bell rang and Aunt Rose rushed to the front door with me following.

There stood three little kids in costume. Their mother smilingly watched them from the sidewalk. "TRICK OR TREAT!" they shrilled.

"Who are you?" Aunt Rose demanded. "You're not from around here."

The kids looked confused. "Oh, we're new in the neighborhood," their mother called up. "We live around the corner on Brier Street."

Aunt Rose grunted and went to get the candy.

I smiled at the kids. They were awfully cute. The biggest one had on a Ronald McDonald outfit but I couldn't figure out the other two.

I asked the older girl what she was supposed to be. "An Egg McMuffin," she said. "My brother is an order of french fries."

Aunt Rose returned, holding up the tray of candy with one hand as if she were the Statue of Liberty holding the torch. "All right now," she said in her bossy voice, "don't be pigs. One piece of candy is enough."

Glancing down at their big trick-or-treat bags, she grumbled, "You'll get plenty of cavities from that junk and diabetes, too."

The kids took one Tootsie Roll each and ran down the stairs. "Better keep an eye on them," Aunt Rose yelled after the mother. "They could get poisoned or kidnapped."

The doorbell didn't ring at all for the next half hour. Aunt Rose couldn't understand why. "Look at that," she said. "I bought so much candy and nobody even comes around."

The poor thing didn't even have a clue.

"Aunt Rose," I began, "did it ever occur to you that maybe you scare the kids and their parents? I mean, you tell them they're going to get cavities and diabetes and they could be kidnapped and all."

She looked at me in surprise. "What do you mean?" she asked. "I'm doing it for their own *good*. I only—"

"—*mean well!*" I chorused along with her.

"Well, most naturally!" said Aunt Rose.

"I told you she'd ruin my social life—and I was *right!*"

"*Now* what?" Donna asked.

I told her the whole embarrassing story as we walked to school the next morning.

". . . and then about eight o'clock, the doorbell rang. Guess who was there, taking his kid brother trick or treating— Chris McConnell."

"Now that," said Donna, "is what *I* call a *treat*. So what happened?"

"Well, first of all, Aunt Rose gave a lecture about candy rotting your teeth. And then she told a story about some lady in her Group who had diabetes and had to have her toes amputated. And then she started in on Chris."

"On Chris? What about?"

I gave a resigned sigh. "She said Chris was too old to be going around on Halloween. She said he ought to be home studying and maybe he'd learn something about arithmetic because he always made mistakes when he was her paperboy."

"Oh, wow." Donna gave me a sympathetic glance. "Did Chris see you?"

"I don't think so. I was hiding in the living room. I was so mortified."

As we turned the corner, who should be walking leisurely in front of us but Mike Matthews.

"Hello, Mike," Donna sang out.

He turned around. "Yo, Donna—yo, Katie." He moved in easily between us.

"Well, Katie," he said to me, "did you have a good Halloween? Your broomstick didn't break down, I hope."

"How much do you charge to haunt a house?" I shot back.

"Come on, you guys," Donna said. "It's too early in the morning for all that clever wit."

"You're right," Mike said. "Want to talk about the essay contest, Katie?"

"What about it?"

"Like what social issue do you think you'll write about?"

"I don't know," I said. "What would you write about?"

"Maybe child abuse," Mike said. "Or teenage suicide."

I looked at him in annoyance. Oh, darn, those were two topics I could really get into. But if I did, Mike could say I stole his ideas.

As we walked along, my mind was racing. I kept thinking of all kinds of subjects for my essay. *The arms race? The drug problem? Teenage pregnancy?*

34

Of course, I would have to do some research in the library before the competition so I'd have some background and—

"Yo, McConnell!" Mike called out.

The name jolted me out of my reverie. There, across the street, was Chris McConnell. He was holding hands with the blond cheerleader.

"I hear Chris and Betsy Russo are going together," Mike said.

A tidal wave of disappointment washed over me. There went Goal #3—at least for now. *Maybe Chris and Betsy won't last very long*, I told myself.

In the meantime, I knew I had to concentrate on Goals #1 and #2. First of all, I needed to do something about my grades so I'd have a better shot at winning the essay competition. Maybe then Chris would notice me!

I thought about my game plan. Instead of hanging around Donna's house so much, I ought to use that time to study, I decided. I'd figure out somewhere comfortable in Aunt Rose's house to work and maybe do extra-credit projects even if I had to do them on weekends and over vacation. There was an added bonus in that—I wouldn't have to listen to Aunt Rose and her Sylvia stories.

"Hey—what's with you, Katie?" Mike asked. "You look like you've seen a vision."

I didn't even realize I had stopped short in the middle of the sidewalk.

Donna was staring at me. "Are you okay?"

"Okay? I am *fan*-tas-tic!" Already I was starting to feel like a winner. Nothing was going to stop me from winning first prize in the Jonathan Waring Essay Competition!

Chapter 5

"Give me one good reason why I should waste a perfectly good day off from school to go to Filene's with Aunt Rose." It was Teachers' Convention Day and I'd been planning to do some research on my essay topic.

"Because," Mom replied, "Aunt Rose says she wants to buy you a nice outfit for the holidays."

"That's a good enough reason," I had to admit.

"I knew my powers of persuasion would win you over," Mom said. "And kindly don't complain about giving up your day off. Don't forget, I'm taking Friday as a vacation day just to play referee for the two of you."

My mother and I were sitting at the kitchen table having a late-night snack, something Aunt Rose did not approve of. She was out for the evening and we were enjoying ourselves, just like old times. Mom and I could laugh and relax and do whatever we wanted without Aunt Rose's nagging us about every little thing. Like eating green apples, for instance, which Aunt Rose doesn't approve of. "They're not good for you," she insists. "You'll get a stomachache, especially if you eat them in the evening."

And although Mom swears she *never* gets stomachaches of any kind, Aunt Rose carries on so much it's not even worth arguing with her.

I discovered that some things are not worth arguing about with Aunt Rose the day she went berserk when she saw me sitting on my bedroom floor.

"You shouldn't sit on a cold floor," she had cried. "You'll get *piles!*"

"Piles of what?" I asked. I honestly didn't know what she was talking about.

"You know what I mean. "Piles—hemorrhoids.""

I had started to laugh. "Aunt Rose, you don't get hemorrhoids that way."

"Hah," Aunt Rose said, getting more upset. "You'll be sorry when you have to sit on a pillow! Marilyn," she called out to Mom, "tell your daughter she shouldn't sit on a cold floor."

Mom had come to my rescue. "Rose, that's an old wives' tale. You do *not* get hemorrhoids that way. I've told you a hundred times, a hemorrhoid is like a varicose vein in your—"

"I don't need such details." Aunt Rose covered her ears. "And I don't care what magazines you read. It so happens I know of someone who used to sit on that stone wall near the library when she was a girl. And believe you me, today she has terrible hemorrhoids—she has to eat standing up!"

Living with Aunt Rose has been a culture shock for me. At least my mother knew what to expect, but I didn't.

It was so good to be alone with Mom, laughing and talking at the kitchen table. I missed our little apartment and the way things used to be so easy and relaxed.

We were in our pajamas and bathrobes, like two guilty little kids, eating our forbidden snacks. Mom was on her second Granny Smith apple, and I had opened the refrigerator looking for the leftover spaghetti from dinner.

Aunt Rose would have been horrified. I mean, if a cold floor could give you hemorrhoids, what would cold spaghetti and meat sauce do to your insides?

Mom and I talked about the upcoming Shopping Safari on Friday. My Panasonic was playing WPEN Softrock. The house, as Aunt Rose would have said, was "all lit up like Broadway." I was really enjoying my cold spaghetti. It tasted even better than it did when Mom had made it for dinner.

Just as I inhaled the last strand, we heard a crunching sound in the driveway as Aunt Rose's big old Buick wheezed up the incline.

Mom leaped from the table and dumped the apple cores into the garbage disposal. I ran and shut off some lights and turned the radio dial to the "sweet show tunes of station WPIL," then quickly rinsed off the spaghetti plate and fork and put them in the dishwasher.

"Your slippers," Mom whispered. "Put them on." That's another of Aunt Rose's crusades. She says people who go barefoot pick up all kinds of diseases and infections.

My aunt was happy to see us. "Oh, you're still up. It's nice having someone here when I get home." She looked around. "Why are all the lights on? And you"—she squinted at me— "what's all that red stuff on your mouth?"

I quickly brushed my hand across my lips to remove the last traces of spaghetti sauce.

"That lipstick is not a becoming color for you," Aunt Rose decided. She sat down at the table, waiting for Mom to ask how her evening was.

"So, Rose, how was your evening?"

"Terrible, just terrible." Aunt Rose brightened right up. "Between Edith Grimes and the new lady—Bella Wing—oh, that Bella, she's very depressing to be with."

"Well, Rose, that's why she's in the Grief Group. Didn't you tell me she'd lost her husband only a few weeks ago?"

"Still and all," Aunt Rose said, "she doesn't have to put on that long face. Oh, and wait until you hear about Edith Grimes."

You'd have thought there was some really hot gossip about poor Edith, the way Aunt Rose leaned forward and started to whisper.

"The thing is, Edith is all set on getting married again. A

week from next Saturday." She paused dramatically. "To Lester Potts—can you *believe* it?"

Mom and I looked at each other. We didn't have the foggiest notion who Lester Potts was.

"She sprung it on us," Aunt Rose continued, "just like that. Edith Grimes is getting married—one, two, three!"

"Maybe," I leered suggestively, "she *has* to get married."

That went over Aunt Rose's head. "No, she doesn't. Edith's husband left her well off."

"Well, I think it's nice," Mom started to say, "if Edith Grimes and what's-his-name love each other, then—"

"Oh, don't be so foolish," Aunt Rose said testily. "Lester Potts is an old coot. He's got a pacemaker, a plastic hip. Who knows what other parts aren't his," she added darkly.

"Love will find a way," Mom quipped.

"Love! Hah," Aunt Rose snorted. "Lester Potts is looking for a nursemaid if you ask me. I told her, 'Edith, the only thing you'll get out of this marriage is a handicapped license plate.' "

"You *said* that to her?" I blurted out.

"Most naturally. Lester Potts doesn't want a wife, he wants a maid. Silly Edith—she'll wait on him hand and foot and he'll still leave everything to his children."

"I hope you didn't tell her that," Mom said.

Aunt Rose looked surprised. "It's for her own *good*. I told her, 'Edith, he'll bury *you* first. He'll be limping across your grave in his walker.' "

Mom groaned. "Rose, if you keep talking that way, they won't want you in the Grief Group."

"Oh, come on now, Mom," I said all sweet and innocent. "Aunt Rose meant well. Didn't you?" I was laying it on thick.

"Well, at least *somebody* in this family understands. And what do you think the payoff was? Did Edith appreciate it?" Aunt Rose asked in righteous indignation. "What do you think Edith said to me?"

Before Mom could answer, I said loudly, "She said, 'Rose, why don't you mind your own business.' "

"That's exactly it!" Aunt Rose said, staring at me amazed. "How did you know? Sometimes I think Kate's got PMS—she reads minds."

"*PMS?*" Mom started to laugh. "Oh, Rose—you mean *ESP*. PMS means 'premenstrual syndrome.' "

"Whatever," Aunt Rose said with a wave of her hand.

On Thursday morning, who should be waiting for us at the corner of Donna's street?

"Oh, darn—not Mike Matthews again," I said. "He's getting to be a regular every morning."

"What of it," Donna said. "He's a fun guy."

"About as much fun as having a root canal." I hoped Mike heard me.

"Hey, there, good-looking," he said. "And hello to you, too, Katie."

I ignored him.

"And how's my literary rival today?" he asked.

"Nobody is your rival," I shot back. "You are in a class by yourself. You have no peer."

"She has a sharp and waspish tongue," Mike said, falling in step beside me. "Next time the Drama Club does *The Taming of the Shrew*, you ought to try out."

"Good idea. And next time they do *Peter Pan*, you ought to try out for Tinker Bell."

Donna hurried to get between us. "Okay, you two. That's enough. No more fighting."

Donna means well, but she doesn't understand that this is the way Mike and I have always talked to each other. Sometimes we have a regular comedy routine going, and we entertain everyone within earshot.

We walked along, making small talk. Then Donna said, "What's new with your aunt Rose and the Griefettes?" That, of course, got Mike all curious, so I had to tell him about Life with Aunt Rose . . . the Curse of the Egyptian Mummy, and the Young and the Restless, alias Edith Grimes and Lester Potts.

Like Donna, Mike was a great audience. He roared as I related my aunt Rose anecdotes. "She sounds great. The perfect role model for you, Kate. You've got a lot in common—you're both critical, bossy, insulting."

I was trying to think of a snappy comeback when Mike added, "By the way, have you picked your essay topic yet? I'm going to the library on Friday to do some research."

"You are? What's your topic?"

"I'm not sure yet. I thought about merit raises for teachers—that would really be a hot subject. Or throwaway kids—that's hot, too."

"Katie is doing her research in Filene's Basement on Friday," Donna joked. "With her aunt Rose, no less."

"That's right," I said as we climbed the seventeen steps of Pennington High School's main entrance. "I'm bound to get inspiration there."

"Hey, another good topic." Mike snapped his fingers. "Why teenage girls are such compulsive shoppers and spenders."

With a little salute, he trooped off to his homeroom.

Chapter 6

"Six dollars' worth of the high test," Aunt Rose told the attendant at the gas station. "And check the air in the tires."

To Mom, she whispered, "You just watch, he'll tell me the tires don't need air."

"The tires don't need air," he called out.

"You see?" Aunt Rose was triumphant. "They always tell you that."

"Well, maybe your tires *don't* need air," Mom said.

"Oh, Marilyn, why do you always believe what people tell you. He's just too lazy to put the air in, that's all, so he tells you the tires are all right."

I was sprawled out in the backseat of Aunt Rose's Buick, my eyes shut. I was still half-asleep, but Aunt Rose wanted to get an early start to Boston. She said everything at Filene's would be picked over if we got there much after ten o'clock.

Aunt Rose paid for the gas and practically made the guy swear an oath that the tires were okay.

"We don't want any trouble on the highway," she told him. "We've got a long trip."

"Going far, Mrs. Cronin?" the attendant asked.

Suddenly, I recognized the voice. I had heard that Chris McConnell was working at Buddy's Sunoco.

I slumped as far down on the backseat as I could.

"We're going to Boston," Aunt Rose said, sounding quite important. "It's a long ride. It'll take, oh, a good hour and twenty minutes."

"Oh, wow!" Chris said in a deadpan voice. "That far!"

His response must have made Aunt Rose do some serious thinking. She turned around and tapped me on the arm. "Katie," she said in her loud voice, "go use the ladies' room before we get on the road."

My face burned with Instant Embarrassment. "I don't have to," I mumbled through clenched teeth.

"You'd better go to the bathroom," Aunt Rose kept on. "You're not a camel, you know!"

Was that a snicker from Chris? I kept my eyes tightly shut, all the while scrunching down even farther.

"For heaven's sake, Rose. Leave the kid alone!" Mom said.

"All right, all right. But it's not healthy to hold it in." Aunt Rose had the last word as she started up the car so abruptly my stomach lurched.

"Have a nice trip!" Chris called out as we careened out of Buddy's Sunoco down the street and onto the highway.

Mom had wanted to drive, but Aunt Rose refused to go in our car, which she says is an old junk that would probably get stuck on the road. She won't let anyone else drive her Buick.

Aunt Rose crept along in the left-hand lane, talking nonstop, totally oblivious to things like signals, shouts, horns tooting, and anyone's opinions concerning her driving ability. She was too busy discussing Sylvia and Sylvia's new boyfriend. Three years ago Sylvia had gotten divorced, and Aunt Rose was dying for her to get married again.

"Did she tell you his name?" Aunt Rose asked Mom. "And why is she always so secretive about everything? She'll tell you, but she never tells me."

That bothered Aunt Rose a lot. Sylvia didn't write to her

very often, but she did write to Mom a lot—long letters in a neat, tiny handwriting. And she always sent them to Mom's office, which must have driven Aunt Rose crazy.

"All I know is, his name is Warren. He's divorced, too, and he comes from Boston."

"I want Sylvia to find someone," Aunt Rose brooded. "And you, too, Marilyn. You should get married again."

A car in back of us had been honking nonstop and riding on Aunt Rose's tail until finally she moved into the right-hand lane. It confused her so much she took the Braintree exit instead of staying on 128 South to Boston.

Of course, to save face, she claimed she had decided to go to Filene's in the South Shore Mall instead of having to fight the Boston traffic.

The rest of the day was about as much fun as having your wisdom teeth out. Aunt Rose decided the stores back home had just as nice things and they cost less, too. She was also upset because it suddenly occurred to her she would miss her soap operas.

"Friday is the worst day to miss your stories," she complained. So while Mom and I poked through Filene's and Jordan Marsh, Aunt Rose found an appliance store in the mall where she could watch at least one of her stories.

Aunt Rose had said she wanted to buy me an outfit. There were some great-looking sweaters and pants, but the outfit that grabbed my eye was a dress. I don't wear dresses that often, but this was a full-skirted turquoise dress with three-quarter sleeves made of rayon, which looks good any season. It was also on sale, which made Aunt Rose quite happy.

"You ought to buy a nice dress, too, Marilyn," Aunt Rose said when she joined us afterward. "All you have is office clothes. You need something to wear on a date."

"A date?" Mom laughed. "I haven't had a date in ages."

"Well, maybe you will," Aunt Rose said, looking quite mysterious and proud of herself.

"See that?" Aunt Rose said as she paid for my dress. "Katie's living with me just a short time and already she's turning into a little lady. She even bought a dress."

Of course, what Aunt Rose and Mom didn't realize was the reason I wanted that dress. It would be perfect in the spring when I went up on stage to accept first prize in the Jonathan Waring Essay Competition.

_____*Chapter 7*

The funny thing is, for all my complaining, it was Mom who started to unravel first.

It happened on the Friday after Thanksgiving. That was the night my mother had a blind date with Mervin Purvis, eligible widower.

"Mervin is a great catch," declared Aunt Rose.

"That's what you said the last time you fixed Mom up on a blind date," I reminded my aunt. "Mom called him a reject from the Twilight Zone."

"Oh, *her!*" Aunt Rose brushed that aside. "What does *she* know? Mervin is settled. He's mature. And he doesn't have any children so he can't leave his money to them. You have to *think* of things like that."

Aunt Rose had been raving so much about Mervin Purvis that I was dying to meet him. He was supposed to pick Mom up around seven o'clock to take her out to dinner.

But when I got home from baby-sitting at six o'clock, Mom and Mervin had already left. I was disappointed.

"You just missed them," Aunt Rose told me. "Mervin decided to pick her up at quarter of six instead of waiting till seven. He says if he eats too late, he gets pockets of gas."

"Pockets of *gas?*" I repeated. "Mervin certainly sounds intriguing."

Aunt Rose was only too happy to fill me in on all the romantic details. My mother had worn her blue dress and her pearl necklace and looked very nice. Mervin even told her blue was his favorite color.

"I tell you, Katie, I'm so excited!" Aunt Rose clattered around the kitchen, cleaning out drawers. "Did I tell you Mervin owns a nice two-family house? Your mother could quit her job and stay home. He's got plenty of money, they say. Who knows, maybe he'll pay for your college."

"Hey, Aunt Rose," I teased her. "They've only gone out to dinner and already you've got Mervin paying my tuition."

Still, the more I thought about it, the more it sounded pretty good. A house of our own, Mom's not having to work, getting my college education paid for. I was beginning to like Mervin Purvis.

Around eight-thirty, we heard Mom's key in the back door.

"Thank you for a lovely evening!" she called out in a loud voice.

"Why are they back so early?" Aunt Rose cried. She crept over near the door to hear what was going on.

There was a cough or a wheeze, most likely from Mervin. Then Mom's voice, loud and clear. "No, Mervin, I'm sorry. Good night, now."

"I bet he wanted a good-night kiss," Aunt Rose whispered. She was straining to hear what was happening on the back porch.

"Oh, Marilyn," she called out sweetly to Mom, "why don't you invite Mervin in for coffee?"

"Mervin doesn't want any coff— What did you say? You do? Oh—well, er . . ." My mother's voice trailed off. Another turn of the key and in she came.

She didn't look very happy.

Behind her walked Mervin Purvis. No, that's not quite right. Mervin did not walk. He *doddered*.

Aunt Rose hadn't done him justice. He was settled and mature, all right. Mervin was a tiny gnome of a man with wispy white hairs that peeped out from under a Zorba-the-Greek hat. He wore a heavy plaid overcoat that was much too big for him, and a sly smile on this thin face.

He took off his cap with a flourish and gave a little bow.

"Mervin Purvis—at your service!" he cackled. "This your daughter? Pretty little gal. Favors you, Madeline."

"It's *Marilyn*," Mom corrected him tersely. "Not Madeline. As I was telling you before, Mervin"—she cleared her throat—"we still haven't been able to find another secretary, so I have to go into the office early tomorrow. I'll just say good night again. Please excuse me." With that she ran upstairs.

Mom and Mervin had obviously not made a Love Connection. But would Aunt Rose give up? Never. She sat Mervin down and fixed him a cup of Postum, all the while babbling about my mother.

"She's a wonderful cook, my sister. She makes a delicious pot roast."

Aunt Rose got so carried away she even started praising *me*. "A *very* intelligent girl, my niece. Not silly or boy-crazy like some."

Hah—if you only knew, Aunt Rose!

After half an hour, it occurred to the two of them that my mother had no intention of coming back downstairs. Mervin stood up, knees creaking, and announced he had to go home. Aunt Rose steered him toward the door. Apparently he didn't see too well either.

"Good night," he sang out. "Good night! Don't let the bedbugs bite!"

"Hoo, Mervin, you're such a card!" Aunt Rose tittered.

"I'll tell Marilyn to invite you over for supper. Maybe you'd rather have meat loaf."

Mervin clickety-clacked down the back stairs. It sounded as if he wore taps on his shoes. A few minutes after we heard him drive off, my mother stormed into the kitchen.

Aunt Rose quickly opened the silverware drawer and started to clean it.

My mother stood in the doorway, watching her. "Rose," she said finally, "how *could* you?"

My aunt didn't answer. She got very busy inspecting the soup spoons.

"Do you know how *old* Mervin Purvis is?" Mom kept on. "Mervin Pervis is almost seventy years old! Did you know that?"

"Yes, but he's a *young* seventy," Aunt Rose said faintly.

"How could you ever fix me up with someone like him? And what a dirty old man he was! He kept pawing me in the restaurant."

"He has a new Oldsmobile," Aunt Rose said, her head bent low as she wiped out the drawer. "And they say he owns a lot of stocks and bonds."

My mother pulled out a chair and sat down. "I was so mortified in the restaurant. Every time the waitress came over, he'd jump up and say, 'Mervin Purvis at your service!' "

"He happens to be a good catch," said Aunt Rose.

"A good *catch*? Then let someone from your Grief Group catch him! I'm throwing him back!"

"Did you hear that, Katie?" my aunt cried dramatically. "Your mother is throwing away your future!"

I shrugged. "Mervin Purvis makes her nervous."

"Your mother is too fussy." Aunt Rose looked at me for support. "Let me tell you, there's women in the Grief Group who'd give their eyeteeth for someone like Mervin."

"Rose," said Mom patiently, "please listen to me. I appreciate what you're trying to do." She took a deep breath. "But I am simply not interested in Mervin Purvis. I have nothing in common with him. He's too old for me."

"You're no spring chicken," Aunt Rose sniffed. "There's mileage on *your* meter!"

"Well, at least I'm still in drive!" Mom yelled. *"Which is more than Mervin can say—he's in neutral!"*

"More like reverse," I said. The two of them turned to glare at me.

"YOU GO UPSTAIRS!" they yelled in unison.

I sat back quietly. I wasn't about to leave. This was getting too exciting.

"And to think," Aunt Rose said, "I only wanted to help—and you don't even appreciate it."

"Please don't help so much, Rose. Please let me make my own mistakes."

Aunt Rose was hurt. "Well, you certainly *did* make your own mistakes all right. That husband of yours for one . . ."

My mother said quietly, "I appreciate what you've done for me, but it doesn't give you the right to run my life." I couldn't believe that was Mom talking. She's always been such a wimp around Aunt Rose.

"Nobody appreciates all I do," Aunt Rose complained. She grabbed handfuls of silverware and dumped them into the sink. Then she turned on the faucet full force. "Not you. Not Sylvia. Not Henry. I used to cut Henry's toenails—but did I get any thanks?"

"We're not talking about Henry, we're talking about *me*. Is this bill *ever* going to get paid?" Mom was hollering above the sound of the water running.

"No appreciation," Aunt Rose muttered. "No thanks for all I've done."

My mother leaped from her chair. "Thanks? You want thanks? All right, Rose—thanks for giving me guilt for the rest of my life."

Aunt Rose scrubbed a steak knife with a Brillo pad.

"And thanks for embarrassing me in front of people. And thanks for being so stubborn and bossy and opinionated . . ."

My aunt wasn't even paying attention. She was picking at a teaspoon.

By now my mom's face was red as a beet. "Oh, and thanks for fixing me up with gassy Mervin Purvis."

"This looks like egg." Aunt Rose frowned at a fork. "Katie, you should be more careful."

"And most of all," Mom concluded, "thanks for not even listening to what I say." She sat down again.

"Well"—Aunt Rose turned to her—"it's about time you thanked me. Everybody needs to feel appreciated."

My mother just sat there, her mouth open, staring at Aunt Rose. "Strength," she said. "Give me strength."

She caught my eye and the two of us started to laugh.

Aunt Rose kept asking what was so funny.

Chapter 8

Donna stood back and looked at me critically. "No, that line is too thick."

She grabbed the mink-brown eyeliner out of my hand. "Here—let me show you."

I shut my eyes tightly while she concentrated on my left eye. "You need to make it narrow, close to the lashes." She turned to Mom, who was sitting on the bed, watching us. "What do you think, Mrs. Williams?"

"I think it's a family problem," Mom said, laughing. "I never could get the hang of putting on eyeliner either."

"It's because this room is too bright," I said. "I can't concentrate with all this whiteness. Maybe we should practice in my mother's room."

"It's too dark there," Mom said. "And besides, you get nervous with George Washington watching you."

"You know, Katie," said Donna, "you really need to practice if you want your eyes to look good for the party."

"Okay. Okay." I took the eyeliner pencil back from her and leaned close to the mirror. I still had my bottom lids to line. "You know, the last time I wore eyeliner, Aunt Rose said I looked like a raccoon."

"Your aunt doesn't like makeup," Donna agreed. "She always tells me I wear too much."

"My sister is a bit old-fashioned," Mom said apologetically.

"Old-fashioned?" I hooted. "That's an understatement. It's more like she was frozen in a time capsule. They haven't defrosted her yet."

"My grandmother is a lot older than your aunt Rose," said Donna. "No offense, but Grams is a lot more modern."

"Donna's right, Mom," I said. "How come Aunt Rose is the way she is?"

My mother sighed. "Rose didn't have it easy. Our mother was sick for a long time so Rose took care of the family. She had to quit school early and go out to work in the mills because we needed the money."

"That's probably why she's so bossy," I mused. "She's used to running things."

Donna had taken a brush out of her cosmetic bag and was fluffing it over her cheeks. Then she carefully outlined her lips.

"How does this look?" she asked.

"What's going on?" From out of nowhere, Aunt Rose had materialized. We hadn't even heard her come home from her luncheon with the Grief Group.

I was so startled my eyebrow pencil swerved and made a big dark line underneath my eye.

"How come you're making those raccoon eyes again?" Aunt Rose wanted to know.

"Don't bother to knock," I muttered. For the zillionth time, I prayed Mom and I would find an apartment or a house of our own—the sooner the better.

"The girls are going to a party next week," Mom explained. "They want to practice getting beautiful."

"Hoo," Aunt Rose snorted, "they'll need a lot more practice, believe you me." She seemed pleased with her joke.

"Oh, Rose, there's a letter for you downstairs from Sylvia," Mom said.

"I know. I saw it when I walked in." Aunt Rose patted a cream-colored envelope. "I was just about to read it when I heard you in here."

"Don't let *us* stop you," I said pointedly. Why does she always have to horn in when my friends come over? Donna seemed to ignore her, finishing her makeup. Nothing ever bothers good-natured Donna.

"The two of you look like chorus girls," Aunt Rose said, shaking her head. "My Sylvia *never* wore makeup."

Mom glanced at her watch and jumped up from the bed. "My goodness, I didn't realize the time. I have to go over to the supermarket. We need to get signatures for the rent review petition."

"Oh, you and that affordable housing business." Aunt Rose made a face. "You'll never meet anyone that way."

"After Mervin Purvis, everything is anticlimactic," I said.

"Oh, *that's* what I was going to tell you. I found out Mervin is seeing Bella Wing. Can you imagine?" Aunt Rose was indignant. "Her husband is hardly cold and she's chasing that old goat."

Now that Mervin wasn't a marriage prospect for Mom, he had become an old goat as far as Aunt Rose was concerned.

"I'll be back around four o'clock," Mom said, "and I'll put the roast in the microwave. It won't take long."

She kissed us all good-bye.

"Hmph," Aunt Rose said to nobody in particular, "you'd think Marilyn was going off to China with all that kissing good-bye."

I thought my aunt would leave, too, but instead she took Mom's place on the bed. Apparently we weren't going to lose her that easily.

"So," she asked, "whose party are you going to?"

"Nobody you know," I answered, hoping to cut it short.

But Donna said, "It's Neysa Johnson's party."

"Who's Neysa Johnson? I can't seem to place that name." Aunt Rose frowned. "Oh, wait, isn't she the little colored girl?"

I groaned. "Aunt Rose, Neysa is *not* a little colored girl. For one thing, she's not *little*—she's five foot eight. And for another thing, she's not 'colored.' Nobody uses that word anymore. Neysa's black."

"It's not *nice* to call someone black," Aunt Rose said, shocked. "And besides, she's not black. I happen to know that family. They're light brown, not—"

"Oh, Mrs. Cronin," Donna cut in diplomatically, "what do you think of this shade of lipstick?"

Aunt Rose examined Donna out of narrowed eyes, then declared, "You look like a Christmas tree."

My aunt turned to me. "Her father is the judge, right? They live in that big house on Hyatt Avenue." She was like a dog with a bone. "And her mother's the schoolteacher, right?" she finished triumphantly.

"Right." I didn't want to discuss anything more about Neysa or her party. The less Aunt Rose knows about anything, the less chance of her sticking her nose into things and embarrassing me.

It so happens Neysa is one of the most popular girls at school. I was *thrilled* to be invited to her party, especially since I'd heard Chris McConnell was going to be there. Best of all, he'd be alone. Chris and Betsy Russo had broken up.

Aunt Rose wasn't quite through yet. "Well," she remarked, "I think it's very nice you have a Negro friend. I used to work with a lovely Negro lady years back in the Nemasket Mills."

We watched as Donna put the finishing touches on her makeup. Donna always buys those magazines that show you how to put on three shades of eye shadow and how to do contouring so it looks as if you have cheekbones.

Aunt Rose looked from Donna to me. "What a pair," she marveled. "One looks like a raccoon and one looks like a Christmas tree."

"Excuse me," I called out loudly. "I'm going outside to tip over some garbage cans. Donna, you come downstairs and we'll stick a star on your head."

Donna burst out laughing.

Aunt Rose looked puzzled. "What did you say?" she asked. "Half the time I don't know what you're talking about."

I changed the subject. "So what's new with Sylvia?" I asked, pointing to the letter Aunt Rose was holding.

"Oh, I'd forgotten all about the letter." Aunt Rose slit open the envelope and pulled out a sheet of cream-colored stationery.

She read the letter slowly, squinting at Sylvia's neat, tiny handwriting. "She says everyone's fine. They've had a lot of rain. Well, they always have a lot of rain there. The twins are fine. They got a new puppy . . . I don't know why they need a dog anyway . . . it's not sanitary . . ."

Aunt Rose shifted her weight and continued, "Oh-ho, listen to this! She's still seeing that man, Warren, the engineer. The boys like him a lot, she says. Aha—they might get married next year! Oh, that's wonderful!"

"Way to go," I said. "Maybe I'll be a bridesmaid. I always wanted to see Oregon."

"It's a mother's prayer answered." Aunt Rose dabbed at her eyes. "Sylvia's been divorced for five years now. Let's hope your mother finds a nice husband, too."

"What did you say his name was?" I asked.

"Sylvia's fiancé? His name is Warren." Aunt Rose squinted at the letter. "It's Warren—OH, NO! NO, IT CAN'T BE!"

Aunt Rose looked pale and shaken. "OH, NO—HOW COULD SHE DO THIS TO ME?"

"What's the matter?" I asked, dumbfounded. "What's wrong?"

But Aunt Rose didn't seem to hear me. She got up and left my room shaking her head. "Oh, no," she kept repeating over and over. "I'll be a laughingstock. She can't do this to me!"

Chapter 9

As soon as Mom walked in the door that afternoon, Aunt Rose pounced on her, waving Sylvia's letter in her face.

"Of all the men in the world, why does Sylvia have to be marrying *him!*" Aunt Rose sniffled.

Mom took off her coat and read Sylvia's letter. "Oh, Rose, that's wonderful. I knew she'd been seeing Warren for quite a while. He sounds very nice."

"Oh, he sounds *nice*, does he?" Aunt Rose countered.

"Yes, he does. He's an engineer, he owns his own home, the twins are crazy about him. What are you so upset about?"

"What am I so *upset* about? Didn't you notice his *name?*" Aunt Rose yelled.

"Of course, I noticed his name," Mom said. "It's Warren, Warren Sylvia—oh, my goodness—" She burst out laughing.

"See *that?* You're *laughing*. My own sister is laughing," Aunt Rose cried in agitation. "Everyone will be laughing. What an awful name. My poor daughter—she'll be *Sylvia Sylvia*."

"Well," said my mother. "It's certainly—*different*."

"It's got a nice beat to it," I offered.

Aunt Rose shuddered. "*Sylvia Sylvia!* It sounds like a rock singer. Or a striptease dancer."

"Aunt Rose," I suggested, "how about if Sylvia uses her

middle name or her middle initial? Maybe that would sound better. What's her middle name anyhow?"

"It's Olivia," said Aunt Rose hopefully. "Sylvia Olivia Sylvia—how does that sound?"

I shook my head. "That's a mouthful. Besides, it spells out 'S.O.S.' It'd be weird having a monogram that's an international distress signal."

Aunt Rose sat down heavily at the table. "I can see it all now," she said glumly. "They'll be laughing behind my back at the Grief Group."

My mother had washed her hands and was fixing dinner. She looked up from the roast she was seasoning. "Rose, you're making way too much of all this. It's ridiculous. In fact, Sylvia is a very common last name around here."

"As long as Sylvia is happy, that's what matters," Mom said.

"But why couldn't she fall for a Smith or a Jones? Anything but Sylvia!"

"Easy for *you* to say," my aunt muttered.

"You want to know what real problems are? You should hear some of the stories I heard today when we were trying to get signatures for the petition."

Curiosity got the better of Aunt Rose. "What stories?"

"Stories about people getting evicted because they can't pay these outrageous rents," Mom said. "One little old lady nearly broke my heart. She's been living in a two-family house for over thirty years. Now all of a sudden her landlord sees what big rents they're getting, so he raises her rent nearly two hundred dollars a month! The poor woman only gets a small widow's pension. She can't *pay* that kind of rent."

"What a terrible thing," Aunt Rose clucked. "I didn't know landlords can do that."

"They certainly can," Mom said grimly. "And they're doing it. Landlords can charge whatever they want to since there's no rent review or rent control board in Pennington."

"What'll happen to that woman?" I asked.

"She'll either have to pay the rent increase or move out. But rents are high everywhere. And there's a big waiting list for elderly housing. Even so," Mom sighed, "you wouldn't believe how many people won't even sign the petition to set up a rent review board."

"Why not?" Aunt Rose asked.

My mother shrugged. "For one thing, the newspaper keeps publishing editorials blasting rent review. They make it sound like it's a God-given right to gouge tenants. And the real estate people are always writing letters to the editor about rent review— they want to keep the rents high. It's good for the real estate market."

"I bet that old lady signed the petition," said Aunt Rose.

"Actually, she didn't. She was afraid to. A lot of elderly people are afraid to sign their names to anything."

"Hah," snorted Aunt Rose. "If I was there, I'd get those old folks to sign the petition, believe you me."

Mom smiled. "I believe you, Rose. If anyone can do it, it's you."

Aunt Rose stood up and took the dinner dishes out of the cupboard. She motioned for me to set the table.

"Getting back to the subject of Sylvia," she said. "I suppose you're right, Marilyn. It's not such a terrible thing."

"Now you're being sensible," Mom said approvingly.

"After all," Aunt Rose continued, "you never know. I might be worried for nothing. Maybe it won't even work out. Maybe she and this Warren will break up. You have to look at the bright side of things."

It was a long week, waiting for Neysa's party, though Donna said it dragged because Mike wasn't walking with us in the mornings anymore. He had been going to school early to work on a special computer project. No doubt getting extra credit for it, I thought enviously, which would push his grade average even higher.

We hadn't seen Chris McConnell walking to school either.

Now that the weather was getting colder, he was probably driving or getting a ride with one of his pals. It was still the highlight of my day when I'd see him in the hall and he'd say "Hi."

On Wednesday of that week, the first issue of the *Pennington Pennant* came out. My editorial, "Cheating Cheats Us All," was at the bottom of page 4. I'm sure hardly anyone read it.

Except Mike, of course. "That would have been a great topic for the essay contest," he said.

And he was probably right—it *would* have been a great topic. Why hadn't *I* realized that?

On Thursday afternoon I stopped off at the main branch of the library to get some material for a report on Emily Dickinson. As I was checking out my books, I spotted Cindy Harrington in the reference room.

I almost didn't recognize her. My mother had been right—Cindy looked so *different*. She was pale and drawn, and dark circles shadowed her eyes.

She jumped up from the reading table when she saw me. "Oh, Katie, I'd love to talk but I have to run now," she said. With that, she grabbed her books and hurried away.

I just stood there, watching her rush off, wondering why she looked so different and why she had acted so cold toward me.

Chapter 10

Friday finally arrived—the night of Neysa's party.

I raced home from school so I would have plenty of time to make myself look good. The most important thing was my hair. I took my time blowing it dry and used everything on it—mousse, gel, scrunch spray—and luck was with me. My hair looked really nice! I even did a pretty good job with the eyeliner, too.

I had nagged Mom into buying me a new outfit—a pale-pink angora sweater and some great-fitting jeans.

Aunt Rose was horrified when she saw what I was wearing. "*Jeans?* You're wearing jeans to a *party?*"

"Sure," I said. "Everybody's wearing jeans." Sometimes I wonder where my aunt has been for the past twenty years.

"Well," huffed Aunt Rose, "I would most certainly never allow *Sylvia* to go to a party in jeans."

My mother was putting on her coat to go to a housing meeting. "Rose, that's what they wear these days. And let me remind you, Sylvia practically *lives* in jeans. Remember how you complained about that the last time she came down for a visit?"

Mom winked at me and waved good-bye as she headed out the door.

That had shut Aunt Rose up for the moment. She was staring at my eye makeup, probably ready to make a comment, when the telephone rang. It was Donna. She wanted to know if Mom could drive us to the party. Donna's parents were supposed to take us there, but they had phoned from the restaurant where they were having dinner to say they still hadn't been served.

"By the time they eat and get here, it'll be *late*," Donna groaned. "All the best guys will be taken."

"Oh, rats," I said. "My mother already left. Unless maybe my aunt could take us."

Even as I asked Aunt Rose, I had a hunch I was going to be sorry.

She was only too happy to oblige.

"I always wondered what the inside of that house looked like," she said. "I heard they fixed it up like Hollywood."

My aunt knows the history of every house in town—who lived there before, what they paid for it, and how much it's worth today.

We drove to Donna's, where Aunt Rose tooted the horn so loudly a neighbor came out on the porch and told her to be quiet. Finally Donna came into the backseat of the car in a cloud of L'Air du Temps. Aunt Rose started to cough. "Pfoo—a person could choke from that smell," she said accusingly.

Neysa's house, imposing brick with a big winding driveway, was in the historic section of town. In the spring and summer the grounds are covered with the most beautiful flowers, and Neysa had mentioned they had a greenhouse since her mother is really into gardening.

"Old Doctor Fenton used to own this house," Aunt Rose informed us, as if we really cared. "Huh—I wonder if they knocked down the wall where his waiting room used to be. He was my doctor."

As we got out of the car, Aunt Rose shut off the engine and opened the door.

"Where are *you* going?" I asked.

"I only want to take a peek at the inside," she said. "Just for a minute."

"You *can't* go inside," I hissed. "Nobody else's relatives went inside."

"How do you know?" she shot back. "It's early yet. There won't be many people there."

"Please," I begged. "Don't go in."

But Aunt Rose kept following us. "Just one little minute," she promised. "I want to see that front room. They wrote it up in a magazine."

I gave up. "All right. But just for a second."

Neysa greeted us at the door. I didn't bother to introduce Aunt Rose. I hoped maybe Neysa would think my aunt was related to somebody else.

I got a glimpse of the living room, filled with pale pink sofas, Oriental area rugs, and masses of plants. To the right was the dining room, where a long mahogany dining room table glistened under a sparkling chandelier.

Aunt Rose planted herself in the middle of the foyer, taking it all in, not missing a single detail. She was in heaven.

"Hoo," she said in a loud stage whisper, "I'd like to have what *this* cost!" Neysa's father, Judge Johnson, was staring at her.

I could feel my face burning. "You said you'd *leave!*" I mouthed.

Donna and I followed Neysa down the stairs to the finished basement, a recreation room nicer than most living rooms. It was paneled in a light wood and had two matching tweed sofas and comfortable chairs. Neysa had decorated the room with pennants and poster-size photos of the basketball team. I spotted Chris in one of them and he looked great.

Neysa's younger sister was walking around with a tray of something that looked delicious.

I was about to reach over and take one when a familiar

loud voice behind me remarked, "Hoo, those buggers are fattening!"

"Oh, no!" Like two synchronized Rockettes, Donna and I whirled around to see Aunt Rose, big as life, standing there, surveying the party.

"What are you *doing* here?" I whispered frantically.

"I'm leaving, I'm leaving." Aunt Rose has this voice that really carries. "I just want to see how they fixed up the cellar."

At that moment Neysa's mother walked by, carrying a tray to the table. Mrs. Johnson is the head of the history department at Pennington Community College.

Aunt Rose eyed Mrs. Johnson, who happened to be wearing an apron over her dress. "What a fancy party *this* is," Aunt Rose said loudly. "Look at that—they even hired a *maid!*"

There was a silence so deafening I wished I could disappear.

Mrs. Johnson handled it with class. "Sometimes I *do* feel like a maid," she said lightly. "I'm Delia Johnson, the party girl's mother. And you are—?"

"Oh, I beg your pardon. Mrs. Rose Cronin," my aunt announced grandly. "I'm Katie Williams's aunt." She pointed to me.

Somehow I managed not to have a stroke.

"Would you like a crab puff?" Mrs. Johnson asked.

"Don't mind if I do," Aunt Rose said, not fazed in the least. "They're so small, I'll take a few—for later." She wrapped a couple of crab puffs in a napkin and put them in her pocketbook.

The room seemed to be filling up with kids. Out of the corner of my eye I saw Chris McConnell, leaning up against the wall.

"Hello, Mrs. Cronin," I heard him say. "Enjoying the party?"

Finally Aunt Rose left. But it was too late. As far as I was concerned, the party was over. Ruined. My face was still red from blushing. Someone even asked me if I was running a temperature!

I was too upset to enjoy myself. It was too bad because there was even live music. Neysa's brother and his friends have this rock group that's terrific and very danceable.

Not only that, there were even more guys than girls—something that doesn't happen too often at parties.

"What's the *matter* with you?" Donna whispered. "Look *alive*. You're like a zombie!"

"I can't help it," I whispered back. "I feel like everyone's looking at me."

Around ten-thirty I couldn't stand being there any longer. I called the house to see if Mom could pick me up. Aunt Rose answered. Her voice sounded strange.

"What's wrong?" I asked. "You sound funny."

"Oh, Katie." I had never heard my aunt sound that way—like she was crying. "The most awful thing happened."

"What's the matter?" I cried, alarmed. "Is it Mom?"

Aunt Rose mumbled something and started to sob. And then the phone went dead.

Chapter 11

Neysa's father drove me home.

I was shaking, terrified that something had happened to my mother.

Over and over, on the way to the house, I prayed, "Please, God, let Mom be all right."

It seemed like an eternity until Aunt Rose answered the door. My hands were shaking so much I couldn't find my key.

I stumbled inside. "What's the matter?" I said, my voice quivering.

Aunt Rose sniffed into her handkerchief.

"Did something happen to my mother?" I yelled. *"Will you answer me?"*

"Your *mother*! Nothing happened to your mother. In fact, that sounds like her car now." We heard the familiar wheeze and squeaky brakes as Mom's old car stopped in front of the house.

"It's what happened to *me* that's terrible." Aunt Rose muffled a sob.

Mom came into the house and stopped in her tracks when she saw Aunt Rose's face. "Rose, what's wrong?"

"Something awful happened," I said. "But I don't know what it is."

My mother shook Aunt Rose's shoulders. "Is it Sylvia? The twins?"

"It's . . . it's . . ." My aunt could barely talk. "It's the Grief Group."

"Something happened to somebody in the Grief Group?"

"Worse than that." Aunt Rose dabbed at her eyes. "They don't want me anymore. They kicked me out."

Mom put her arm around Aunt Rose, who kept sniffling as she related the details. "It was that Bella Wing who started it all. She came over with a couple of others. They said I'd been in the group longer than anybody else. They said seven years was too long and it was about time I resolved my grief. Can you imagine that?"

"Oh, Rose. That's awful. You must feel terrible."

"Well, most naturally, I feel bad," Aunt Rose snapped. "I can't go on the bus trips anymore, I can't go to the potlucks. They don't want me anymore."

"They'll be sorry," Mom said loyally. "You'll find another group. And they'll appreciate you more."

"Nothing will ever be as much fun as the Grief Group," Aunt Rose said mournfully.

"If it makes her feel any better, she's not the only one who's miserable," I told Mom later on when we were upstairs. "I had an awful time at the party." I told Mom what happened with Aunt Rose.

My mother sighed, something she's been doing a lot more of since we moved in with Aunt Rose. "What can I say? That's the way Rose is. Underneath, she really has a heart of gold."

I felt even more depressed the next morning when Donna called to tell me the party was terrific and she had met a really cute guy.

"You should have come back when you found out everything was all right at home," she said. "Chris McConnell was sitting alone most of the night. It would have been the perfect chance to talk to him."

"I was too embarrassed to come back after the way I rushed out of there," I said, feeling miserable, jealous, furious—you name it.

The more I thought about it, the madder I got. I stormed into Mom's room and slammed her door. "Aunt Rose is ruining my social life—what little there is of it," I said angrily. "I can't take much more of this. Promise me we'll be out of here by the summer."

Mom didn't answer right away. Finally she said quietly, "Katie, I can't promise that."

I flopped down on her bed and put the pillow over my eyes. "It's bad enough during the school year," I said, "but at least I'm out of the house until three o'clock Monday through Friday. What's it going to be like in the summer—home all day with Aunt Rose? At least if I were sixteen I could get a full-time job."

When the going gets tough, the tough get going. I jumped off the bed.

"Where are you going?" Mom asked.

"To write some letters," I said, feeling better now that I was taking charge of my life.

I sat down and wrote to my father in Atlanta. And after I finished, I wrote a letter to Grandma and Grandpa Williams in Delray Beach, Florida.

I asked them all if I could spend next summer with them. Maybe Dad and my grandparents would both invite me down, so I could spend part of the summer in Atlanta and part of it in Florida.

Just thinking about being away from Pennington and Aunt Rose made me feel better.

In December, there was a two-week spell of gloomy weather. Rain and more rain fell, then rain and snow, rain and sleet, and there seemed like an eternity of gray skies.

My grandmother sent me a letter saying they didn't think

71

it was a good idea for me to visit them next summer. For one thing, it was awfully hot in Florida. For another thing, their condo was small. Besides that, they were planning to spend a month in Connecticut visiting Aunt Louise. And furthermore . . .

I got the message. Maybe it was for the best, I told myself. After all, staying with your grandparents could be pretty dull.

Anyhow, I'd much rather visit my dad in Atlanta. I kept hoping I'd hear from him.

"I hate this weather," Donna complained as we trudged home from school. A biting wind kept turning our umbrellas inside out. "I can't wait for Christmas vacation—Fort Lauderdale, here I come!"

"You're so lucky," I said enviously. "I wish I were going someplace warm."

"It'll seem weird going swimming at Christmastime," Donna said.

"Oh, just grit your teeth and bear it. Think about me when you're lying in the sun. I'll be at the library, doing a paper on Elizabeth Cady Stanton."

"Another paper? How come you're doing a paper over vacation?"

"Because," I said, "I need the extra credit to push up my grades." At least all my studying and extra work was paying off—all my grades had gone up.

I stopped off at Donna's for a snack only to find out she was on a diet kick. "I told my mother to cut up some fresh veggies," she said, taking a platter of celery, carrots, broccoli, and cauliflower out of the refrigerator. "I need to lose some weight so I can fit into my bathing suit."

"Life isn't fair," I decided as we chomped on some carrot sticks. "You'll start off the New Year looking tan and thin. And I'll be pale and fat. No, let me correct that—I'll be pale, fat, and crazy. Aunt Rose will probably drive me nuts over vacation."

"How's Rosie doing?" Donna asked. "Is she still upset about getting kicked out of the Grief Group?"

"Upset? Devastated is more like it," I said. "The worst thing is, she doesn't have anywhere to go anymore so she's always around the house. At least when she was in the Grief Group, she was out a lot. Now it's like she's on twenty-four-hour call indoors."

"Oh, wow." Donna bit into a broccoli floret and made a face. "She needs something to keep her busy."

"Tell me about it," I groaned. "Now that she has all that time on her hands, she insists on doing the cooking!"

"Your *aunt* is doing the cooking? She's such an awful cook." Donna started to giggle. "I'll never forget the time she invited me over when she made that fish loaf."

"She made it again last night," I said. "It was *grotesque!*"

"Well," Donna said, "I think you better figure out something else she could join so you can get her out of the house again."

"That," I said, "is my resolution for the New Year!"

_____*Chapter 12*

The only good thing I could say about Christmas vacation was that living with Aunt Rose made it seem a whole lot longer.

Not *better*. Just *longer*.

Either she dragged around the house, or she would get these wild fits of energy and clean everything in sight. She tackled the attic and the basement. She took all the dishes out of the cabinets and washed them even though she had done that just before Thanksgiving.

Then she decided to do some baking for the holidays.

She pored through Mom's cookbooks and found a recipe for "Easiest-Ever, Can't-Fail Christmas Sugar Cookies."

They failed. Those cookies were so awful even Aunt Rose wouldn't eat them.

The worst thing was, she insisted on doing the cooking every night.

"I can't take much more of this," I whispered to Mom as we were cleaning up after dinner. "I mean, how can Aunt Rose ruin *steak*? It tasted like *shoe leather*!"

"That's because she won't broil it," Mom whispered back. "She always cooks steak in the frying pan."

I loaded the dishwasher, feeling sorry for myself. What a

75

nothing vacation this was. And I didn't even have Donna around to complain to.

Aunt Rose wandered into the kitchen. "I think I'll cook a turkey for Christmas dinner this year," she announced.

"You mean we're not going to Cousin Elaine's?" I blurted out. Aunt Rose and Mom are very close to Elaine, their only cousin in town, and we usually have Christmas dinner at her house.

"Not this year," Mom said, not meeting my eyes. "She and Bill are going up to Nashua to see the kids. I guess I forgot to tell you, Katie."

Aunt Rose was going on about what she planned to serve. "I'll make a nice roast turkey and—"

"*No, not turkey!*" Mom and I cried in unison. The last time Aunt Rose served turkey, she hadn't cooked it all the way through so it was pink inside and quite disgusting.

Aunt Rose snapped her fingers. "You're right, turkey is too dry. I'll make a nice roast chicken and—"

The thought of Aunt Rose's cooking was enough to galvanize Mom into action. She ran over and grabbed the newspaper. "Rose," she said firmly, "you need to get involved in some kind of activity to keep yourself busy."

"Nothing will ever be like the Grief Group," Aunt Rose said wistfully. "They always had so many things going on."

"You'll find something better," Mom said as she scanned the calendar listings. "Let's see, there's square dancing—no, that's for couples. There's the Great Books Discussion Group— no, that's not for you. Hmmm, maybe you could take some kind of course at the YWCA after New Year's."

"How about a cooking course?" I suggested, but I said it under my breath so nobody heard me.

On Saturday, Aunt Rose decided to take down all the curtains and wash them.

I decided to make tracks and go Christmas shopping. I was

almost done except for Aunt Rose's gift. "I don't know what to get her," I said to Mom. "What does she *like*?"

"She doesn't like *anything*," Mom said, "so it doesn't matter *what* you give her—as long as she can return it. Rose likes to return things. It gives her something to do."

I browsed through the mall, picking up some last-minute things—a manicure kit for Donna, a roll of wrapping paper, and ribbons.

I had already mailed my out-of-town gifts so they would arrive in time. I had gotten some place mats for my grandparents and a two-pound box of butter crunch candy for my dad.

Mom had taken care of sending presents to Sylvia and the twins. Donna and I would be exchanging gifts when she got back from Florida. For Mom, I had bought a peach-colored polyester blouse that looked like silk and some cologne.

Snow flurries started to fall as I walked home from the bus stop, and it put me in such a holiday mood I started whistling "Jingle Bells."

But when I walked into the house, I stopped whistling. Something smelled awful.

"What's that smell?" I said, choking.

"It's a new recipe," Aunt Rose informed me proudly. "Chicken livers with ziti."

I took one look at those chicken livers congealing in the Corning Ware and nearly gagged.

When Mom got home, she had the same reaction. "I'm certain this is delicious, Rose," she said, choosing her words carefully, "but, uh, Katie and I are allergic to chicken livers. I think I'll just fix us tuna fish sandwiches."

"Since when are you allergic to chicken livers?" Aunt Rose demanded suspiciously.

Luckily the phone rang. Aunt Rose picked it up, still grumbling about how hard she had worked cooking dinner and what did we expect her to do with all those chicken livers anyhow?

"Hello—hello? *Who?*" A look of utter astonishment came over her face. "*Who* do you want? *Katie?* Who's calling?"

"Is that for me?" I got up from the table and went over to the telephone.

Aunt Rose wasn't about to let go of the receiver. In a tone of wonder she announced, "*It's a boy—he's calling Katie!*"

I practically had to force the receiver out of her hand. "Hello?" I managed to say, all out of breath.

"Katie? It's Mike here."

Oh, *no!* It *would* have to be Mike Matthews. I waited for him to make some wisecrack about Aunt Rose and how she was carrying on, but Mike just made small talk. Like whether we'd get snow for Christmas, how he wanted to do some cross-country skiing, and whether I'd finished my shopping.

All the while, Aunt Rose stood in front of me, gesturing wildly. "Is he asking you for a date?" she wanted to know.

I put my fingers to my lips, motioning for her to be quiet.

"Anyhow," Mike went on, "the reason I'm calling is, I wondered if you'd like to see *Annie* tonight at the university. My father got some free tickets."

He caught me by surprise. I was about to say "Sure, I'd like that" when Mike said, "I know this is kind of last-minute on a Saturday night. But I figured, well, I'd call anyhow—maybe you wouldn't be busy."

What exactly did he mean by that? Was he putting me down? Come to think of it, he had some *nerve* calling me at five-thirty on a Saturday—as if he expected me to be sitting around doing nothing. Maybe he'd already asked some other girls and they had turned him down.

"Thanks, Mike," I said coolly, "but I've got plans for this evening."

"That's too bad. Maybe some other time." He actually sounded disappointed.

Even before I hung up the phone, Aunt Rose was peppering me with questions.

"Who was that boy? Did he ask you out for tonight? And what kind of plans do *you* have, I'd like to know."

"I have plans to watch the Saturday night movie on Channel Thirteen," I told her loftily.

My aunt clapped her hand to her head. "Did you hear that, Marilyn?" she called to Mom. "Your daughter is so popular she's turning down dates."

Mom was busily chopping celery for the tuna fish salad. "I can't tell Katie whom to go out with."

"Of course you can!" Aunt Rose clucked indignantly. "That's what mothers are for!"

_____ *Chapter 13*

As it turned out, I didn't watch the Saturday night movie after all.

Mom had gone up to her room to draft a letter to the newspaper asking people to support the rent review petition.

Aunt Rose had decided to sort out some old snapshots and put them into albums. She sat down next to me on the sofa, arranging the photographs in two piles.

I was about to turn on the TV set when she waved a snapshot in front of me. "Look at this, Katie—that's me in front of the old Harkum Mill. Wasn't I nice and thin back then!"

I stared at the yellowed photograph. It was hard to believe that once upon a time Aunt Rose was young and smiling and not wearing a girdle.

"Oh, and look at this one." She turned the picture over to check the date. "Oh, my, this was when we went on strike."

"On *strike*? You mean you belonged to a labor union?"

"Well, most *naturally* I was union! We were all union. Union got us decent wages. Union put food on our table. That's how people today got pensions and medical benefits—because of the unions!"

I looked at the photographs with growing interest. We had been studying the labor movement in social studies.

"Did you ever go out on a picket line?" I asked.

"Hoo, *did* I!" It was as if I had touched a nerve. Aunt Rose started to talk and couldn't stop. She told me about the big textile strike years back and the time the union organizers came to Lily Jay Manufacturing. She told me about the people she worked with. She even sang the old union songs.

"We used to sing them while we walked in the picket line," she recalled. "The boss thought we wouldn't stay out there—it was so cold you could freeze your head off. But nobody left that line. We stuck together and we won."

She picked up the other pile of photographs. "These are the family pictures," she said. There were endless snapshots of Sylvia as a baby and toddler . . . Uncle Henry scowling into the camera . . . family scenes with different relatives . . . pictures of Mom when she was little.

"Hey, who's this?" I picked up a photograph of a girl in a long dress. "She looks like me."

"Well, most naturally. She *should*. That's your grandmother. You're the image of her."

"I am?" I kept staring at the photograph. "I never knew I looked like my grandmother. I've hardly ever seen pictures of her."

"Well," said Aunt Rose, "when she died, your mother took it terribly. Night after night, we'd hear her crying herself to sleep. She never wanted to look at pictures or talk about Mama, even to this day."

"I don't know anything about my grandmother," I said slowly. "What was she like?"

"Oh, she was something." Aunt Rose smiled in recollection. "Always full of little jokes and stories. You're a lot like her. You even sing off-key the way she did."

Another floodgate had opened. Aunt Rose leaned back and started to talk about the old days—anecdotes about both my grandparents and other relatives. "Marilyn was a change-of-life baby. When she was born, your uncle Jack and I were already grown up."

I hung on every word. These were things Mom would not and could not tell me because she was too young when her mother died. And I think she's blocked out a lot of memories because they're too painful to talk about. But now, thanks to Aunt Rose, I was finding out so much I had never known about my family. It gave me a new sense of connection.

"I love hearing this," I said in wonder. "It's like my very own *Roots*."

Aunt Rose handed me a picture. "You can keep this one. You really look so much like Mama here—the way your eyes crumple up when you smile."

"*Crumple?* Don't you mean *crinkle?*"

"Crinkle, crumple, what's the difference?" Aunt Rose shrugged. "Don't forget, *I* didn't graduate high school, you know."

I looked at my aunt, and all of a sudden I had a brainstorm. I knew what I was going to give her for Christmas. Something that would be perfect for her. Something she wouldn't return the day after Christmas!

My mother had been warning me that we were on an economy binge and that I wouldn't be getting much for Christmas. But she always says that. On Christmas morning there were a bunch of gifts from Mom under the tree. She gave me a sweater, a jacket, makeup, books, stationery, and a fluffy pink beret and matching scarf.

My grandparents had sent me a check, and Dad had given me earrings.

Sylvia's gift was a cable-knit ivory wool sweater she had knit herself. I had to admit it was gorgeous. "That daughter of mine," Aunt Rose bragged, "she can do anything."

Mom loved the gifts I got her. She opened Sylvia's gift—a periwinkle-blue hand-knit sweater like mine.

"Here," Aunt Rose said, handing me a box. "And be careful—don't rip that wrapping paper. I can use it again next year."

I was careful opening the present so I wouldn't rip the paper. Inside the box was a flannel nightgown that looked unbelievably itchy. There was also a pair of slipper socks that were the wrong size. And the gift of gifts—an ugly wool bathrobe, the kind you see in movies, except old men are usually wearing them.

Her gift to Mom was an equally ugly nightgown and some thermal underwear.

"I bought those the day after Christmas last year," she informed us. "That's when you get the best bargains."

Aunt Rose opened Mom's gifts. The gloves and purse would, we knew, be returned the next day as soon as the store opened.

Aunt Rose took the package I handed her. "Now what did Katie get me? I wonder," she said.

She took the paper off carefully and stared at the box inside. "A *tape recorder*?" she said, puzzled. "What do I need with a tape recorder?"

"So you can do an oral history," I said. "You can talk into the recorder and tell what it was like when you went to work in the mills and all about the labor union and the strikes and—"

"Katie, what a wonderful idea!" Mom cried. "How did you happen to think of that?"

"We talked about it in social studies. Our teacher said we should tell our grandparents to record oral histories."

Aunt Rose was all excited. "You want *history*? Hoo, *I'll* give you history. I could tell stories that would curl your hair."

We had dinner around one o'clock. Aunt Rose bustled around wearing a white apron and waving a big wooden spoon.

"So far, so good," I whispered to Mom as we nibbled on celery and olives. "She didn't ruin these."

Mom frowned and shushed me.

"All right, here we go now!" Aunt Rose yelled as she carried the platter of roast chicken to the dining room table. Well, at least it looked cooked.

We passed around the candied carrots, cranberry sauce, a bowl of mashed potatoes with world-class lumps, and some grayish gravy.

I started to cut my chicken. And cut and cut. The knife didn't seem to do a very good job. I speared a piece of chicken on my fork, popped it into my mouth, and started to chew.

And chewed and chewed.

It was like trying to eat rubber. I glanced at Mom. Her jaw was going up and down, up and down.

I raised the napkin to my mouth and daintily spit out the chicken. I noticed my mother furtively doing the same.

"Dig in," Aunt Rose told us. "There's plenty of chicken."

"Um, Rose," Mom said brightly, "what, er, exactly did you *do* to the chicken?"

"Oho, you like it, huh?" Aunt Rose was beaming. "Well, I learned my lesson that time when I didn't cook the turkey long enough. This time, I cooked the chicken a nice long time so it would be tender."

"What temperature did you cook it on?" Mom persisted.

"Oh, I didn't cook it in the oven. I put it in the microwave," Aunt Rose said, sounding quite proud of herself. "And I even cooked it for half an hour longer than it called for. I wanted to make sure it got done."

"No wonder." Mom shook her head. "Rose, you should never cook anything too long in the microwave. It gets rubbery. And especially cooking it half an hour longer than—"

"There's nothing wrong with that chicken," Aunt Rose snapped. "It looks fine to me." She bit into a piece and nearly lost her upper plate.

We all busied ourselves passing around the other dishes.

"Well," Mom said, trying to smooth things over, "at least the candied carrots are all right."

The fact is, they were *undercooked*—still hard in places. It was not what you would call Great Moments in Dining. We finished the rest of the meal in silence.

"What's for dessert?" I said deadpan. "Wax fruit?"

Mom glared at me and jumped up to get the dessert in the kitchen. I was glad about that—who knows how Aunt Rose might ruin the Sara Lee pie that was sitting on the counter.

The rest of the day was nice and relaxing. We cleaned up and went out for a walk. My grandparents called me from Florida and we talked the usual three minutes. Then Sylvia called and put Warren on the phone. He wished us all a merry Christmas. Even Aunt Rose had to admit he sounded nice.

Later on Mom and I were in the middle of a hot Scrabble game when we heard Aunt Rose in the kitchen, talking into the tape recorder. We couldn't make out what she was saying, but then she played it back on full volume.

"Testing . . . testing . . . This is Rose Cronin giving an oral history. This is about the days when I worked in Lily Jay Manufacturing . . . Well, they had this union man from New York—his name was Arnold something-or-other . . . Well, he was carrying on with Millie, the bookkeeper . . . She didn't think we were wise to her . . . They said she used to have a thing for Leo, the shop steward . . . Oh, and one of the bosses, Mr. Steiner, had this bleached-blond wife and whenever she . . ."

My mother and I looked at one another.

"Somehow I don't think Rose has quite gotten the hang of this oral history thing," Mom said with a sigh.

Chapter 14

The main branch of the Pennington Public Library has a really nice reading area. It's set up like a cozy living room with a thick rug, tables, lamps, and big, comfortable chairs.

I was going through the card catalogue when I spotted Cindy Harrington. She was curled up in one of the chairs, a book on her lap. I wasn't sure if she was really sleeping or just pretending so she wouldn't have to talk to me.

Why has she been trying to avoid me lately? Once and for all, I decided to find out.

I walked over to her. Luckily there weren't many people in the library, probably because it was the day after Christmas.

"Cindy," I said loudly, "I want to talk to you."

Her eyes flew open, startled. She really *had* been sleeping. I pulled over a straight-backed chair and sat down.

"Look," I said, "are you *mad* at me or something? The last time I saw you here, I felt like you were avoiding me. What's *wrong?*"

Cindy put her book on the table and sat up slowly. "Oh, hello, Katie."

"My mother said you tried to avoid her, too," I kept on. "Why?" It wasn't just that I was hurt by Cindy's behavior, I liked her as a friend and I was really concerned that something was very wrong.

Suddenly Cindy's blue eyes were brimming with tears. "I'm sorry. It's not you, honestly. I just don't feel like talking to anyone these days."

Cindy had always been outgoing and bubbly. Now it was as if she were a shadow of herself.

"What's the matter?" I asked, puzzled.

It's a good thing they let people talk in the reading room, because once Cindy got started, she couldn't stop. "Things were good for a while," she told me. "We were renting that duplex in the North End and we really liked it there. But then the house was sold, and the new landlord decided to raise the rent $150 a month. So we had to get out."

Her voice broke. "Only there wasn't any place for us to *go*. Either the rent was too high or they wouldn't rent to a family with three kids."

She shut her eyes. "Finally we had to go to the shelter downtown. Oh, God, it was awful."

I was stunned. "Cindy," I managed to say, "I had no idea. Where did you finally get an apartment?"

"We didn't," she said. "We're living at the Pineview Motel."

"The Pineview Motel?" I couldn't believe it. The Pineview was a seedy, run-down place on the outskirts of town. Everyone made jokes about it.

"It's the only place they could find for us. We're on the emergency housing list, but there's a lot of others ahead of us."

"Isn't there someplace else you could stay?" I asked. "With your relatives maybe?"

She gave a harsh laugh. "Our relatives—that's a joke. My uncle Phil and his wife won't even let us do our laundry at their house—let alone *stay* there."

I didn't know what to say. For the first time I realized that Mom and I were lucky to have Aunt Rose. Suppose she hadn't taken us in? Where would we be? At the Pineview Motel, too? Suddenly I understood how frightening it was to be homeless.

"There's four of us in one room," Cindy went on. "We're

all on top of each other. And Mom is so depressed when she comes home from work. She's always crying. That's why I come to the library—just to get away."

By now a couple of people had come into the reading area and were giving us annoyed looks.

I grabbed Cindy's arm. "Let's go get a hot chocolate somewhere—my treat."

The two of us checked out our books at the desk and walked outside. There was a little coffee shop down the street.

We sipped our hot chocolates slowly. Cindy couldn't stop talking. "There's a guy at school I really like," she confided. "He invited me to a school dance, but I told him I couldn't go." Her voice cracked. "I mean, how could I let him pick me up at the motel?"

I didn't know what to say. Cindy asked me how Mom was. She didn't know we had moved out of Fairview Downs and were living with Aunt Rose.

"You're lucky," Cindy said. "To be in a real house, I mean. And it's a nice section of town, too."

"I guess I *am* lucky," I said slowly. "I never looked at it that way."

Cindy glanced at the clock on the wall. "I'd better be getting back. I told Tommy and Jen I wouldn't be out too long."

"I haven't seen them in ages," I said. "How are they doing?" Tommy was twelve and Jen was ten. They were really nice kids.

"Right now they're probably killing each other. Lately all they seem to do is fight." Cindy buttoned her jacket and gave me a lopsided smile. "Well, it's been nice talking to you, Katie. Thanks for the hot chocolate."

"Wait," I said impulsively. "Listen, Cindy—could I go back to the motel with you? My mother can pick me up on her way home from work."

"Why do you want to go there?" Cindy stared at me. "To see how the other half lives?"

"I don't know why," I admitted. "But it's important for me to go there." I told Cindy about Mom and the Coalition for Affordable Housing.

She shrugged. "All right. Maybe it'll do some good if people know what's happening. But I'm warning you, it's a long ride there and the buses don't run very often."

Cindy was right. We waited nearly an hour in the cold, and the ride seemed endless. On the way, I told Cindy about how Mom was trying to set up a Rent Review Board.

"Tell your mother if she wants to know firsthand what it's like in a homeless shelter, we could tell her a few choice things," Cindy said grimly.

The bus lumbered on. We fell silent, staring out the window. Finally the bus came to the edge of town where the divided highway began.

"PINEVIEW MOTEL," the driver called out. Cindy jumped up. "Come on, Katie." As we walked off the bus, the driver and a couple of passengers smirked at us.

"God, I hate that driver." Cindy's cheeks were flaming. "Did you notice that's the only stop he announces? He does that all the time. It makes me feel so *dirty*."

In the drabness of the late-winter afternoon, the Pineview Motel looked even seedier than usual. It was a one-story building, painted pink. Two of the letters in the sign were missing, so it spelled out "INEVIEW OTEL."

Down the road was a used-car lot and an electrical supply store. Past that was a McDonald's. It seemed so desolate.

Cindy and I had to race across a busy divided highway to get to the motel. I called Mom from a pay phone near the front desk and asked her to pick me up when she got out of work.

She was pretty upset to learn where I was. "Katie, you be careful," she told me worriedly. "I'll be there by five-thirty. Don't go outside that room until you see my car."

Cindy and I hurried to Room 104. "The kids had sore throats today, so my mother wanted them to stay inside." She shook her blond curls. "I had to get out. I can't stand this place."

She pounded on the door. Jennifer unlatched the chain, saw me, and shrieked,"Katie! What are *you* doing here?"

"She came to interview us for *Lifestyles of the Rich and Famous*," Cindy told her sister.

"Hi, there, Jenny Penny." I gave her a hug.

"Well," said Cindy, "you wanted to see it, and here it is— home sweet home."

My heart sank as I looked around. Even with an overhead light and a lamp on, the room was dark and drab. There were two double beds with ribbed orange spreads, two dressers, a desk, and a nightstand. The carpet was a brown tweed and the walls a dull beige. In the dressing area, clothes were jammed up against each other. A TV set was blaring.

"Where's Tommy?" I asked as I took off my jacket.

"In the bathroom. He'll be right out," Jen answered.

Cindy went over to the TV set and shut it off. "God, why do you play this so *loud*? I can't hear myself think."

She and Jen started to argue. Cindy wanted the TV set off and Jen turned it back on. Just then Tommy came out of the bathroom.

"Hey, look who's here, Tommy," Jen said. "Remember Katie from Fairview Dumps?"

"Hi." Tommy's glance slid away from me. Like Jen, he looked pale and drawn. He went over to one of the beds and climbed under the covers.

"How's your throat?" Cindy asked. "Any better?"

"What do you care? You never stay around. You just run off all the time."

Cindy didn't answer. Tight-lipped, she drew the drapes and began to straighten the room.

Jennifer sat down on the rug where a Monopoly game was in progress. "Come on, Tommy, let's finish this game."

"I don't feel like it," he mumbled.

"That's not *fair*! Just because I'm winning—that's why you don't feel like playing," she protested.

Before another argument could develop, I sat down on the floor and said, "I'll play for Tommy."

"Aw*right*!" Jen grinned happily. "I've got all the good property and the money. See, I've got a monopoly on the yellows. Tommy didn't have much of anything."

It was a boring game, but I played so as not to disappoint Jen. Cindy sat cross-legged on the floor nearby, her eyes flicking to the TV set and then back to us.

Jen had two houses on Atlantic and Ventnor Avenues and two on Marvin Gardens. Naturally I landed on Marvin Gardens and had to pay her a bundle.

"If you don't own any property, you're doomed," I sighed as I moved my blue plastic token around the board.

"That's such a depressing thought," Cindy said. "It's just like real life."

At least Jen was enjoying the game. "Wait till you come around, Katie," she chortled. "I'm gonna get you *good*!"

I shook the dice and landed on Community Chest. I had to pay $75.

"I'm buying another house," Jen announced. "On Marvin Gardens."

"Uh-oh." I shook the dice and landed on Kentucky. So far so good. On my next turn, I wasn't so lucky.

"I give up," I groaned. "No way I can stay in this game. I can't pay that rent."

Cindy had shut off the TV set and was watching us play. "It's too much like real life," she said.

"I know what you mean," I said, nodding. "Like, no matter what, there's no way we can get ahead. We keep going around and around, landing on someone else's property. And the rents keep going up all the time. We just seem to keep landing on Marvin Gardens."

Nobody spoke. Jen leaned over and swept everything off

the board. "I don't want to play this game anymore. Let's watch TV."

I put the tokens and money and property cards back in the Monopoly box. The four of us watched an old movie in silence. Cindy passed around a big bag of potato chips, absently popping them into her mouth. When we were friends living in Fairview Downs, I never saw Cindy eat junk food. Maybe that was why she looked so puffy now.

I glanced around the room once more and there were so many questions I wanted to ask. *What did you do for Christmas? What do you eat? Where do you cook?* As far as I could see, there was no hot plate, no refrigerator.

As if in answer to my question, Jen said, "Mother called. She's bringing home Kentucky Fried."

"Again?" Cindy made a face. "I'm so sick of it."

On the dot of five-thirty, I heard a horn tooting. I looked outside and saw Mom's car. "There's my chauffeur," I said. "It was good seeing you guys."

Cindy hugged me. "Thanks, Katie," she said. "I'm sorry if we acted weird. It's just—" She couldn't finish.

"It's all right," I said awkwardly. "I understand."

The headlights of my mother's car looked bright and warm and safe as I ran out of the Pineview Motel into the winter darkness.

As we drove home, I suddenly knew what I was going to write about for the Jonathan Waring Essay Competition.

Chapter 15

"I *hate* January," Donna said as we trudged through the snow. "I'm starting a campaign to eliminate it from the calendar."

"You've got my vote," I said. "January sure isn't *my* favorite month."

I held her books while she blew her nose. "Ever notice nothing *good* happens in January? My tan is almost gone, I can't get rid of this cold, and they're predicting a blizzard over the weekend."

Just then someone grabbed my elbow. I whirled around to see Mike Matthews with a big grin on his face.

"Lucky ladies, you have the pleasure of my company this morning. No computer project till Monday. Mr. Howland is out with the flu."

In no time at all, Mike and I were into our usual routine of insulting each other.

"You're *right*, Donna. Nothing *good* ever happens in January," I said, pointing to Mike.

"You don't fool me, Katie," Mike said. "I know you lust after me. You want my body, admit it."

"No *body*," I said, "wants *your* body. Not even for medical research."

"Speaking of research, I came up with three great topics for the essay contest."

"Really? I only came up with one. But you only need one to win."

Mike shook his head. "You know, Donna, since she started to pull up her grades, she's become arrogant."

Donna laughed. "Are you worried about the competition, Mike?"

"Nah, that's the way I like it," he said. "It's just like old times."

We were walking to our lockers, joking around, when Chris McConnell came by. His cheeks were red from the cold and it made his eyes look even bluer. Funny how just seeing someone you like can make your day.

"Hi, Chris," the three of us chorused.

"Hey," he said.

Did I stare at him too long? Did I smile at him too brightly? Mike must have sensed something because he gave me a funny look.

"They say you should be careful what you wish for," he told me, "because you might get it."

I turned to ask him what he meant, but he was already walking down the hall to homeroom.

I stayed after school that day for a meeting of the newspaper staff. Jill Reisman, the editor, assigned me to do a story about Mr. Meacham, one of the most popular teachers in school. "You're a good writer, Katie," she said. "I know you'll do a good job."

That put me in a happy mood. Until I got home. There was a letter from my dad sitting on the kitchen table. He wrote that it wouldn't be a good idea for me to visit Atlanta over the summer. He didn't give any reason. He didn't even say, "Maybe some other time."

I used to feel close to my dad, even after he and Mom got

divorced. But things changed once he got married again and moved to Atlanta. He doesn't write very often anymore, and he's never invited me to visit them.

I threw the letter away. Then I went up to my room, wrapped myself in my yellow comforter, and had a good cry.

Cindy Harrington is right, I thought to myself. *Not all your relatives come through for you.*

I wondered how Cindy was doing. I had called her at the motel a couple of times, but she hadn't wanted to talk.

"It's not you, Katie," she explained. "I don't even want to talk with my friends from school. I feel too depressed. Maybe once we move into our own place, I'll feel better."

Thinking about Cindy made me feel ashamed. I sure was a lot luckier than she was. Maybe my grandparents and my father hadn't come through for me—but Aunt Rose had.

At least I was living in a nice home in a decent neighborhood. I had my own room, my own bed. I had somewhere to be alone and cry.

I wondered where Cindy went when *she* needed to cry.

"You won't believe what happened at work today," Mom said, yanking off her scarf. "My boss informed me that one of our clients complained to him about the letter I wrote to the newspaper the other night."

"You mean the letter about rent review? That was a good letter," I said loyally.

"I'll say," Aunt Rose agreed. "You told those palookas a thing or two."

"That's the trouble," Mom said worriedly. "This client owns a lot of property around town. He certainly doesn't want rent review—he's making a fortune. He told Mr. Farnham if I didn't stop writing those letters, he'd take his business to another firm."

Aunt Rose was outraged. "That's *blackmail!*" she sputtered. "They can't tell you how to live your life!"

"Maybe not," my mother said quietly, "but they could make my life pretty unpleasant."

"Mr. Farnham wouldn't . . . *fire* you, would he, Mom?"

"*Fire* her? Just let him *try*!" Aunt Rose roared. "Marilyn, you tell that bald-headed old buzzard Farnham to mind his own business!"

My mother and I turned and stared in surprise at Aunt Rose. "You can't let those galoots step on you! You've got to stand up for yourself!"

"It's not that simple—" Mom started to say, but Aunt Rose interrupted.

"You march into that office tomorrow," Aunt Rose went on, "and you tell that old fruitcake you're not going to kowtow to any rent-gouging slumlord. And if he doesn't like it, you tell Farnham it'll be a lot easier to get a low-life client than a crackerjack legal secretary!"

Which is exactly what Mom did.

The next day she came home grinning from ear to ear. "It worked, it worked!" she cried, grabbing Aunt Rose and dancing her around the kitchen. "I won! I caught Mr. Farnham by surprise. I told him he was violating my civil rights. I said he should be ashamed to represent a sleaze like Jason Prentiss. And I told him I was seriously considering offers from another law firm."

"You had offers from another law firm?" I asked in surprise.

"No," Mom admitted, "but it sounded like the right thing to say."

"So what happened?" Aunt Rose asked. "Get to the point."

Mom giggled. "First he apologized. He said he was only joking. Then he begged me to stay on—and he even offered me a twenty-dollar-a-week raise!"

With that, Aunt Rose and I clapped loudly. Mom stood up and took a bow.

"Well," she said, "it's one small step for Marilyn Williams. And one giant step for affordable housing."

"I'm going to make it two giant steps for affordable housing." And I let her in on the secret I'd been holding close to my heart. "That's the topic I'm going to write about for the Jonathan Waring Essay Competition."

Mom was ecstatic. "Katie, that's *wonderful*! We'll get so much good publicity that way. I've got plenty of material I can give you."

"Okay," I said. "But I don't just want to talk about statistics. I want to write about how the lack of affordable housing affects real people here in Pennington. Like Cindy and her family."

"That sounds great," Mom said. "Do you have a title in mind?"

"Yup," I said. "I'm going to call it 'Landing on Marvin Gardens.'"

Chapter 16

"Well, how did it go?" I asked as Mom and Aunt Rose came into the house, stamping the snow off their boots.

I looked at their tight-lipped faces. "*Uh-oh*. That bad, huh?"

Mom had been trying to get Aunt Rose involved with some kind of group. She had decided to try Overeaters Anonymous. "Not that either of us is really overweight," she explained carefully. "But we can always stand to lose a few pounds. I've heard they're a wonderful support group."

Aunt Rose yanked off her hat. "Hah, they don't weigh you, they don't tell you how to lose weight, they don't . . ."

"Rose, I keep *telling* you, O.A. isn't like Weight Watchers. The people at O.A. offer support. They share their experiences."

"They ought to share some *diet* tips," Aunt Rose huffed. "That lady with the red hair, she looked like Two-Ton Tillie!"

"You missed the whole *point*. And what did you say that got her so upset?"

"I don't know why she was so mad," Aunt Rose said. "I told her she had a pretty face but nobody could see it under all that fat."

Mom buried her face in her hands. "Rose, the poor woman *knows* she needs to lose weight. That's why she's there."

"Well, if she knows it, let her *do* something about it," Aunt Rose shot back. "She says she's been going there for two years. What a success story. All she did was get up and talk for fifteen minutes about her husband—you'd think he was force-feeding her."

"Oh, by the way," I said, trying to change the subject, "what happened with that senior citizens club you were going to check into?"

"*Those* stiffs? The Pennington Forever Young Senior Citizens—hoo, what a laugh. I went there yesterday and you could grow a beard—that's how slow they play bingo. I tried to tell them how to play, but they wouldn't listen."

"I rest my case," Mom said with a sigh. "You just can't walk in and tell people how to run things."

"Well, I did it for their own good!" With that Aunt Rose stalked off to watch television.

I sat down at the kitchen table across from Mom and opened the *Pennington Daily Dispatch* to the Calendar page. This was becoming a ritual. "We have to keep trying," I said. "Tonight had to be the worst dinner ever. Aunt Rose didn't finish cooking the macaroni. It was like eating walnut shells."

"Poor thing," Mom said. "She's bored and lonely. I tried to get her interested in the Coalition for Affordable Housing, but that didn't work out either."

"Wasn't she thinking about delivering Meals on Wheels?"

"She decided against it. She'd miss her favorite soap operas."

My mother kept looking through the Calendar section. "There must be some group that would appreciate what Rose has to offer."

"There is," I snickered, "but the Marines won't take old ladies."

Mom gave me a reproachful glance. "Let's see . . . Doll and Miniature Collectors . . . no . . . Ski Club . . . no . . . Unitarian Church Singles . . . no."

"Can I take a look?" I pulled the paper over and went

down the list. "Band Parents of Pennington . . . nope . . . American Businesswomen's Association . . . uh-uh . . . Caretakers of Elderly Parents . . . no."

Then, suddenly, the words leaped right off the page!

"*That's it!*" I shrieked. "The answer to our prayers. How come we never thought of it before?" I circled the item in red ballpoint ink.

My mother read it and gasped. " 'Neighborhood Crime Watch—be the eyes and ears of the Police Department.' Katie, it's perfect."

"It's made in heaven," I agreed.

The problem was, Aunt Rose refused to try it. "No more groups for me," she insisted. "Not after the way they threw me out of the Grief Group—like an old dog."

"It'll be good for you. You need something you can contribute to," Mom told her.

"I'm sick and tired of contributing. Let them contribute to *me*."

"You *need* something," Mom said.

"I don't need anything or anyone," Aunt Rose retorted.

"Maybe not," I put in, "but they need *you*, Aunt Rose."

It was the right thing to say. My mother beamed. Aunt Rose sort of twittered. "Well, I don't know . . ." She wanted to be coaxed.

"There's a meeting this coming Thursday at seven o'clock," Mom said, showing her the listing on the Calendar page. "I'll go with you. Please say you'll give it a try."

"Oh, all right," Aunt Rose gave in. "I'll go, but I don't intend to enjoy myself."

Mom winked at me.

My interview with Mr. Meacham went well. I was a little nervous at first because I had never interviewed anyone before, but he put me right at ease.

Gerald Meacham teaches history, and everyone says he's

terrific. I hope I get him when I'm a senior. Even though he's pretty young, he's confined to a wheelchair because he's crippled with arthritis. But that doesn't stop him from doing anything. He started up the Commission for Citizens With Disabilities, and he speaks to all the groups and organizations in the area about the problems of the disabled.

I thought I'd feel sorry for him, but as we talked, I forgot he was crippled and in almost constant pain. He's really upbeat, and he's married, has a couple of kids, likes to travel, and lives as normal a life as you can live in a wheelchair.

Somehow while I was interviewing Mr. Meacham, he managed to turn the conversation around, and I found myself talking about me. I told him that Mom and I had to give up our apartment and move in with Aunt Rose.

"It sounds like quite an adventure living with your aunt," he said.

"An *adventure*?" I echoed. "Why do you call it an *adventure*?"

"Think about it," said Mr. Meacham with a smile. "What does the word 'adventure' mean? It refers to an unusual undertaking that involves excitement, venture, risk."

"The risk part is right," I agreed. "You ought to taste my aunt's cooking."

We finished the interview and I put my notebook and pen away. "It was really a pleasure meeting you," I told him, and I meant it. Just talking with him made me feel good. Mr. Meacham was such a great guy he made me feel ashamed of the way I always complain about things.

That night I told Mom what Mr. Meacham had said about it being an adventure to live with Aunt Rose.

"You know," I said thoughtfully, "if you look at it the way Mr. Meacham does, it almost makes everything sound like *fun!*"

Chapter 17

As I walked into the kitchen, I could hardly believe my eyes.

My mother was layering lasagna!

"You're *cooking*!" I whooped. "Happy days are here again!" I lowered my voice. "Where's Aunt Rose?"

"She's out doing errands. They asked her to be in charge of refreshments for the Crime Clinic."

"Who *says* 'crime doesn't pay'?" I chortled.

Mom slid the pan of lasagna into the oven. "Well, I must admit it certainly perked Rose up."

It was a miracle. Aunt Rose was back to normal. Or abnormal, as the case might be.

"Anyhow, maybe she'll stop watching me and start watching the neighbors," I said.

"She already has," Mom said. "One of the neighbors called to complain that Rose was spying on them."

There was a banging on the back door. I opened it and in rushed my aunt, loaded down with shopping bags. "Can't stay—I'm going right back out to Zayre's—they're having a sale on paper plates. I just wanted to get my coupons." She was all out of breath.

I hadn't seen her so happy since the days of the Grief Group.

"What about dinner, Rose?" Mom asked.

"Who can even *think* about dinner? I've got so much to do. You wouldn't believe all the work that's involved in the Crime Clinic."

"I guess that means Mom has to do the cooking from now on, darn it," I said with mock dismay.

"Well, most *naturally*," Aunt Rose replied. "You'll have to manage without me. I can't slave over a hot stove all day. I'm very busy." With that, she collected her coupons and rushed back out.

Aunt Rose certainly took her Neighborhood Crime-Watching seriously.

Maybe *too* seriously. The Shattucks next door were quite insulted when Aunt Rose mistook their son-in-law for a burglar.

She was also keeping an eye out on the new people down the street. "Something seems fishy about them," she said. "One day I heard their little girl crying something terrible. I think there's child abuse going on."

Aunt Rose really got into crime prevention. She had all the locks changed. She put a sign in the front window that said BEWARE OF DOG, thinking it would scare off any would-be burglars. She also got involved in Project Identification and brought home the special pen the Police Department provides for marking valuables and appliances. "You put your social security number on your things," she explained. "That way, if they're stolen, you can identify them.

Mom and I got lectures about how we needed to sharpen our powers of observation so we could be aware of suspicious activities.

Aunt Rose's obsession was a little annoying, but it was a lot better than listening to Sylvia stories. Life with Aunt Rose was back to normal, and things were looking up for me, too. I had achieved one of my goals—all of my grades were improving. I had just finished my piece on Gerald Meacham, and Jill and the editorial staff loved it. I felt pretty optimistic about the essay contest. The subject of affordable housing was getting a lot of attention lately. As for Goal #3, it didn't seem likely that Chris McConnell was going to ask me out anytime soon. I wasn't sure he even knew my name!

I couldn't believe the essay contest was only a few weeks away. I was so preoccupied thinking about it as I walked home from school one afternoon that I didn't notice the excitement on Hemlock Street at first. But then I saw the neighbors gathered in little groups in the street, and parked in front of Aunt Rose's house was the news van from Channel Thirteen and a police cruiser.

Now what? I thought as I raced up the front steps.

Chapter 18

"Your aunt is a heroine. She saw a robbery in progress and reported it. We caught him red-handed." Officer Griffin, the Police Department adviser for Aunt Rose's Crime Watch group, was beaming proudly.

"In broad daylight," Aunt Rose chimed in. "That palooka was bold as brass."

There was a television camera set up in the living room. I recognized Tracee Taylor, the anchorwoman on Channel Thirteen. She tossed her blond head and said, "Let's try it once more, Mrs. Cronin."

Aunt Rose wasn't the best subject for a TV interview.

"I was looking out the kitchen window minding my own business," Aunt Rose said, "when what should I see but some big galoot carrying a television out of Old Man Moody's house."

Tracee instructed Aunt Rose not to say "big galoot" or refer to her neighbor as "Old Man Moody."

Aunt Rose rolled her eyes in exasperation and started again. "Anyhow, I got suspicious. He didn't look like a TV repairman, and he didn't have a truck or a van either. Furthermore, Mr. Moody is pretty tight with a buck, and he'd never spend that kind of money to fix up a TV set—when they take it to the shop, they charge you an arm and a leg."

Tracee kept blowing tufts of her platinum hair every time Aunt Rose flubbed the interview. Officer Griffin looked on, mopping his forehead every few minutes.

They were certainly going to have a tough job editing that segment. Especially the part where Aunt Rose got carried away and kept yelling, "Bums! Hoodlums! They should go get a job instead of stealing from decent people!"

That night we watched the local news, but Aunt Rose must have ended up on the cutting room floor. Instead, the story showed story showed Tracee Taylor interviewing Officer Griffin about the new Crimebusters Program in which a woman who belonged to Crime Watch saw a suspicious incident and reported it to the police.

"This is a shining example of how Crime Watch inspires citizens," Officer Griffin said. "We need people to act as the eyes and ears of the Police Department. Too many people are afraid to even call us when they see something suspicious. Too many people won't bother to get involved."

He didn't even mention Aunt Rose's name.

Mom and I were so mad we wanted to call up the TV station, but Aunt Rose said not to bother. "I don't care. Anyhow, Officer Griffin said I might get nominated for Watchdog of the Month."

Later on, when we were having tea and Mom's chocolate crunch cake, Aunt Rose confided, "You know, I don't even miss the Grief Group anymore. They were a bunch of crybabies. Crime is a lot more fun than grief."

My aunt wasn't the only celebrity in the family. Mom's picture was in the paper when she gave a talk on affordable housing to the Pennington Women's Club. She always had a fear of public speaking, so it was quite an accomplishment for her.

"Were you nervous?" I asked, plopping down on Mom's bed. Aunt Rose had gone to a Crime Watch meeting, so Mom and I had a quiet evening at home together to chat.

" 'Nervous' is not the word," she said. "At first I didn't seem to be reaching them. But then I started talking about how things would be for their children and grandchildren. I asked if they thought their kids would be able to find a decent apartment or buy a house. I asked them if they thought their grandchildren could afford to live in Pennington or whether they'd have to move away. I told them rent review was an investment in their future. When I finished, they gave me a big ovation."

"One of these days you'll be on the lecture circuit," I told her. "My mother is a genius."

She stopped creaming her face and looked at me. "Katie," she said, "if I'm so smart, how come I'm just a secretary?"

I stared at her. "Mom, what do you mean?"

"I'm not sure. All I know is, I want to *do* more, *be* more."

"What do you want to do? Or be?"

She tissued off her cold cream slowly and sat down next to me on the bed. "I've been thinking about taking some courses to become a paralegal. That's like a lawyer's assistant. Remember Louise, the Spanish girl who used to work in our office? She went to school nights and now she's a paralegal with the Senior Citizens Law Project."

"Then go for it," I said. "I always told you you should, and I'll help you any way I can."

"We'll have to watch our pennies even more than usual," Mom said. "I never realized how expensive it is to go to school at night. It's a good thing we're living with Rose. Otherwise, I could never swing it."

I squeezed her hand. "You'll do it, Mom. You've got the right stuff."

She smiled. "You've got the right stuff, too. I bet you'll walk off with first prize in the essay contest. Isn't it coming up pretty soon?"

"In a few weeks. Did I tell you they're supposed to print the winning essay in the *Daily Dispatch*? If I won, wouldn't it be great publicity for the housing coalition?"

"It sure would," said Mom. "Which reminds me, speaking of housing, I forgot to tell you I tried calling Cindy Harrington's mother. We wanted to have her speak at one of our meetings. But they said the Harringtons moved out."

"Maybe they finally got an apartment. Cindy said they were on the waiting list."

A few days later, as Mom was going through the mail, she handed me an envelope postmarked from a town in Maine I'd never heard of. "Who do you know there?" she asked.

"I don't know *anybody* in Maine," I said as I tore open the letter.

Dear Katie,

You may have tried calling the motel and wondered what happened to us.

Well, believe it or not, we're up here in the wilds of Caribou, Maine, staying with my grandfather. My mother just couldn't stand living at the motel, and they said it was going to be a long wait till they found us an apartment. I don't know which is worse, living at the Pineview or living up here—my grandfather is very strict and set in his ways.

I miss Bishop Reardon and the people back in Pennington. The kids at school here are not very friendly. Oh, well, I'll have to grin and bear it. Jen and Tommy send regards.

Love,
Cindy

PS—You can't believe how cold it's been up here—even at this time of the year. Caribou is up near Canada.

I showed the letter to Mom. "It's not fair!" I cried. "They all hated Maine. Cindy's mother didn't even like going there to visit. She never got along with her father."

There was no return address on the envelope. I wondered if I would ever hear from Cindy again.

"I'm glad we didn't have to move far away to another state," I said. "I guess we were lucky."

Mom put her hand over mine. "Yes," she said. "We were lucky."

112

Chapter 19

"You better set your alarm clock," I told Mom. "Just in case mine doesn't go off."

My mother laughed. "Don't worry. We won't let you oversleep."

I checked my bedroom. Everything was in readiness for the essay competition the next morning. My clothes were all laid out—my comfortable baggy jeans, my lucky red shirt, and my gray cardigan in case it was cold. On my desk were six nicely sharpened No. 2 pencils and six black-ink medium ballpoint pens.

Aunt Rose kept shaking her head as she watched my preparations. "There wasn't this much commotion when they wrote the Declaration of Independence," she snorted.

The telephone rang a few minutes later as she was putting on her coat to go out with her new friends from the Crime Watch. "It's for you, Katie," she called as she headed to the front door.

I hardly recognized the voice on the phone. "Katie, it's me—Neysa," she croaked. "I have a terrible cold."

Neysa Johnson. I had been trying to avoid her ever since the party. I still felt embarrassed every time I remembered what Aunt Rose had said to Neysa's mother that night.

"I've been out for two days with this cold," she said, coughing all the while. "I missed the big English assignment. I figured you could explain it to me. I wanted to work on it over the weekend."

"Oh, sure, Neysa. Hold on, I'll get my notes."

I gave her all the details of the report we had to do. Then we talked for a couple of minutes and she wished me good luck on the essay contest.

"Uh, Neysa," I said, taking a deep breath, "look, I kind of owe you an apology about the way my aunt Rose carried on at your party."

"Hey, Katie," Neysa said, "your aunt doesn't have anything to apologize for." She sneezed and continued, "Oh, I admit I was kind of annoyed at her, too. But then my father recognized her name."

"Recognized her name? What are you talking about?"

"You mean you don't know that story?" Between sneezes Neysa proceeded to tell me something I had never heard before.

After we hung up, I repeated the story to my mother. "Oh, goodness," she said, "I'd forgotten all about that. I was pretty young at the time, but I do remember people talking about it."

I sat on Mom's bed under the watchful eyes of George Washington. "People sure can surprise you," I kept saying over and over.

The next morning, Aunt Rose came into my room bright and early to wake me up, even before the alarm clock went off. "I wake up like a rooster," she said. "I don't need an alarm clock."

I took a nice long shower, hoping it would help get my creative juices flowing. Then I went downstairs where Mom had prepared a huge breakfast . . . bacon and eggs, hot chocolate, and homemade apple muffins.

"I wanted Katie to have an extraspecial breakfast this morning," she told Aunt Rose.

"Hah, you're stuffing her up like a *pig*," my aunt commented. "She'll eat so much, she'll fall asleep in the middle of writing."

The competition was going to be held in the study hall at school. I could have walked there, but Mom insisted on driving me.

As I left the house, Aunt Rose gave me a peck on the cheek and told me, "I hope you break your legs."

"Rose, I think what you mean is 'break a leg'—like they say in the theater," Mom said, chuckling.

"Whatever." Aunt Rose shrugged. "Good luck."

Most of the kids were already waiting outside the study hall when I arrived. Mike Matthews sauntered in a few minutes later. We stood around, joking and laughing, trying to hide our nervousness.

Everyone was certain the topic would deal with a social issue, and they had their essays practically memorized. One girl, whose father is a local police officer, said she was going to write about the drug problem in town.

I started to feel worried. There were a lot of good ideas. Maybe mine wasn't so great after all.

And then suddenly it was time to go inside. We filed into study hall. It looked huge and forbidding on a Saturday morning. Mrs. Tyler, the head of the English Department, explained the rules. We would be given the topic. We could do a rough draft on scratch paper and then copy it over on the white, lined paper. The essay should run no more than three handwritten pages.

There were two other teachers acting as monitors. Mr. Nichols, who teaches science, stood at the back of the room, arms folded, watching us. Mrs. Wetzel, my English teacher, passed out a supply of paper and an instruction sheet to each of us.

"Please do not turn over the instruction sheet until I tell you to," Mrs. Tyler said. "Be sure to write your name, address, and homeroom on the upper left-hand corner of the first page. And put your name only in the upper left-hand corner of each subsequent page."

She gave us a frosty smile. "Should you have any questions, please raise your hand and one of the monitors will come over to you. And now," she continued, "you may turn over your instruction sheet. Good luck."

The instructions were brief and easy to understand. The writing would be judged on originality, content, grammar. I skimmed over that part and went on to the topic.

I couldn't believe what I was reading. Neither could anyone else apparently. There was a collective gasp in the room.

Mrs. Tyler's cool voice cut into the tension. "I understand there were rumors concerning the essay topic. The primary purpose of the Jonathan Waring Essay Competition is to foster creative thinking. With that in mind, let me again wish you good luck in your endeavors."

I felt like crying as I read the topic over once again. It said:

Tell us about an unsung hero or heroine you know who has made a meaningful contribution to the community and why that person deserves recognition.

Across from me, Donald Leung was chewing on a pencil. I stole a look at Mike. He was mopping his forehead, looking grim. Well, at least *that* was a consolation—he was having as tough a time as I was trying to figure out what to write.

My mind was a blank slate. Was there a trick to the essay? The ideal person to write about was someone like Jonathan Waring himself. Was that what they wanted? I reread the topic. No, it couldn't be. Jonathan Waring was *not* an unsung hero.

116

Then I had a brainstorm. What about Gerald Meacham, the teacher I had interviewed for the school paper? He had certainly made a contribution to disabled people. I started to write, then suddenly put my pen down.

Gerald Meacham was very well-known. He wasn't an unsung hero either. And besides, I had already turned in the story about him to the school paper and that might disqualify me.

As the clock on the pale gray wall of the study hall ticked away, I kept getting more nervous and upset. I looked around and everybody seemed to be busily scribbling.

Wasn't there some way I could use all the material I had read on affordable housing? It's too bad Cindy's family had moved away . . . maybe I could have written about them. . . .

Or what about my mother, for that matter? After all, Mom was active in the Coalition for Affordable Housing. So were the other members, though. *Was Mom an unsung heroine. . . ?*

I started three essays and tore them all up. For a few minutes I sat there thinking. And then I started to write.

It was not the kind of essay that would win, I knew, but it didn't matter. I just kept on writing and the words poured out of my heart, easily and naturally.

Chapter 20

"March is the *worst* month of the year," Donna said. We walked home from school, heads bent against the raw wind.

"You said that about January," I reminded her.

"No, March is worse. March is *sneaky*. You have a couple of nice days and then *wham*—it's winter again."

Icy drops of rain began to pelt us. "We'll get soaked!" Donna cried.

Suddenly a horn tooted and a car pulled up alongside us.

Mike's familiar voice called out, "Katie! Donna! Need a ride?" We didn't even know whose car he was in. We just ran over and hopped in gratefully.

Imagine my surprise when I realized we were sitting in the backseat of Chris McConnell's old Datsun. Betsy Russo sat close to Chris, her arm possessively on his shoulder. She didn't look very pleased that Chris had stopped to pick us up. I knew Mike must have asked him to.

"Does everyone know everyone?" Mike asked. "This is Katie and Donna. You know Chris and Betsy. Everyone knows Chris and Betsy."

Chris stopped at the light. He turned around and gave me

a quizzical look. "Katie, is it? I know you, but I can't place where I know you from."

I wasn't sure what to answer. Should I say something like, "Well, you helped carry my things into Aunt Rose's house and she slammed the door in your face." Or, "Remember me from Neysa's party when—"

Chris snapped his fingers. "Now I remember. It was at some party. Mrs. Cronin was there. She's your aunt, right?"

"Guilty," I said faintly.

Just then Betsy Russo broke into the conversation, changing the subject. Betsy apparently didn't like Chris's talking to me. I had heard she was the jealous type.

Mike started kidding around about how crowded it was in the backseat with three of us squashed together.

"Watch where you put your hands, Katie," he joked. "I'm not that kind of guy."

"If we sit any closer, we'll be engaged," I kidded back.

Donna got out first. Mike and I kept up our routine, and Chris seemed to get a kick out of it.

"Katie *lusts* after me." Mike pulled my hat over my eyes. "She's always lusted after me."

When they dropped me off, I rushed inside the house, not even taking off my coat as I dialed Donna's number.

The two of us analyzed every second of that ride.

"I tell you, Chris has his eye on you," said Donna, always loyal.

"Really?" I thought so, too, but I wanted to hear it from someone else.

"Are you kidding? I saw how he kept sneaking peeks at you in the rearview mirror."

I remembered the way Chris had smiled at me and I felt a surge of happiness.

Who knows, maybe the next time he breaks up with Betsy, he might ask me out.

Maybe Goal #3 would come to pass after all.

I sure had bombed out with Goal #2. Every time I thought about the Jonathan Waring Essay Competition, I felt depressed.

A few minutes later, Aunt Rose came home. She asked me if I could help her make a sign for the Crime Watch meeting that night. "Maybe you could draw a burglar climbing out of a window," she suggested.

"Are you serious? I can't draw at all," I told Aunt Rose. "I don't have one drop of artistic talent."

She was disappointed. "Sylvia can draw wonderful. If she was here, she'd whip something right up. You should see how she can draw and paint."

Somehow that was the final Sylvia straw. I just couldn't take it anymore. After Aunt Rose left for her Crime Watch meeting, I cornered my mother, who was folding laundry in the den.

"I'm sick," I told her.

"What's the matter?" she asked worriedly.

"I have a chronic case of Sylvia-itis," I said. "I am sick and tired of hearing about how perfect Sylvia is. Sylvia sings like an angel. She paints like Michelangelo. She can knit and sew and she got all A's and—"

I flopped down on the sofa next to Mom. "I don't mean to be mean, but I'm getting an inferiority complex on account of Sylvia."

"Whoa," my mother said. "Back up. What's this about Sylvia singing and painting and getting all A's?"

"You never have to listen to it, but I do. How come Aunt Rose never brags about Sylvia when *you're* around?"

Mom smiled. "Probably because I know that most of the things Rose brags about aren't true."

"You're kidding!" I cried. "You mean Sylvia isn't the world's most perfect human being?"

Mom stopped folding the towels. "Sylvia is a nice, average person. It so happens she *does* knit and sew quite well. But she's certainly not artistic. And she never got all A's. She actually wasn't much of a student. And as for her singing, she could carry a tune, but that's about it."

I stared at Mom. "You're *kidding!*"

"Don't you know Aunt Rose by now?" Mom asked gently. "She embroiders the truth a bit sometimes. She sees things the way she'd like them to be."

I kept shaking my head. "This is too much. I mean, here I was wondering if there was anything I could do better than Sylvia."

"Lots of things. Including the fact that you get along so well with Aunt Rose. Sylvia never did. The two of them always fought like cats and dogs."

I was speechless.

"I know Rose brags that she and Sylvia are close," Mom went on. "But that's just wishful thinking." She put down the towel she was folding. "You know, I used to feel guilty about it. I felt maybe it was my fault."

"Your fault? Why?"

"Because," Mom said, "I wondered if maybe Sylvia resented me when I came to live with them. I worried that she felt I was taking Rose away from her."

"If anything, Sylvia was probably grateful," I pointed out.

Mom nodded. "I know. Sylvia told me that."

This was all too much for me to digest. I remembered something Mom had said a moment ago. "You really think I get along good with Aunt Rose?" I asked.

"Oh, you get along with her beautifully," Mom said. "Better than Henry or Sylvia or me."

"Are you serious? Aunt Rose drives me *crazy.*"

"Maybe so. But you seem to handle her so well. The two

of you never really fight or argue. She's always bragging about you, too."

My jaw dropped open. "Let me get this straight. Aunt Rose brags about *me*? To who?"

"To whoever. The Grief Group when she belonged to it, the Crime Watch, the neighbors, the relatives."

I started to laugh. "Wouldn't it be funny if Aunt Rose brags about me when she writes to Sylvia!"

Chapter 21

"Do you realize we're celebrating an anniversary?" Mom said. She had just finished baking some lemon nut cookies for Aunt Rose's Crime Watch meeting that night.

"What anniversary?" I asked, my mouth filled with a warm cookie.

"You and I have been living with Aunt Rose exactly six months," Mom said. "Don't you remember—we moved here the end of October."

"How could I ever forget?" I joked. "Well, like they say, time flies when you're having fun."

"It seems as though so much has happened in these six months," she mused.

"That's true," I said. "I'm living with two celebrities. My mother is the famous rent review advocate, and my aunt was the runner-up for Watchdog of the Month."

Mom ruffled my hair. "And my daughter, the writer, did a wonderful editorial in her school paper about homeless kids. Everyone says that's what helped get the City Council to act on rent review."

"It would have been more wonderful if I could have written that for the essay contest instead," I said glumly.

"Why do you keep saying you won't win? You don't know that."

"Trust me, Mom. I know. I didn't even have a *clue* what to write."

"So what or whom did you end up writing about?"

I sighed. "It was so dumb. I don't even want to say. You can read it when we get the essays back. They're going to have each essay printed and framed."

"That's very nice," my mother said. "Isn't Awards Night coming up soon?"

"In a few weeks. To tell you the truth, I don't even feel like going."

"Now come on, Katie." Mom lifted the cookies off the baking sheet and put them on a platter. "Don't be so negative. Be positive."

"You're right, Mom. I positively do not feel like going to Awards Night." I stole another cookie and pinched her cheek. "Gotcha!"

"Yo, Donna. Yo, Katie." Mike waved to us as he crossed the street.

"Well, well. Spring has sprung," I remarked. "Looks like El Braino is back with us." I wouldn't admit I was kind of glad to see him.

"Is your computer project finished?" Donna asked when Mike caught up with us.

"Finito," he said. "And now you two visions of loveliness can again experience the pleasure of my company."

"Let us give thanks," I intoned, "for this great blessing."

The conversation eventually got around to Awards Night. "I'm sure not expecting to win," I told Mike. "I don't even feel like going to Awards Night."

"Neither do I," Mike said. "But they expect us all to show up. You know, when we're seniors, we'll probably be applying for the Waring scholarships and the committee just might hold it against us if we didn't show up for the essay awards."

"Leave it to you to think of something like that," I said. "Speaking of essays, now that it's over and done, tell me—who'd you end up writing about?"

"That was tough," Mike said. "I racked my brain trying to think of an unsung hero who made a contribution to the community. I ended up writing about Mr. Eberstadt."

"Mr. *Eberstadt*?" Donna echoed. "Norman Eberstadt, the *band director*? What did that old lecher contribute to the community?"

"Well, he got the band new uniforms. And he improved them so much they won second place in the state competition. And besides"—Mike shrugged—"I couldn't think of anyone else to write about."

"It *was* a tough topic," I agreed.

"I bet I know what unsung hero *you* wrote about, Katie," Mike said with a leer. "It was me, wasn't it?"

"Oh, darn," I quipped. "You spoiled the surprise."

That day at lunch we heard that Chris McConnell and Betsy Russo had split up again. That was the good news. The bad news was that he was already seeing someone else, a mousy little freshman named Lori Ann Baines.

Within a week, the stories started to circulate. In no time, jokes about Lori Ann were being whispered all over school.

"That locker-room talk is disgusting," Donna said indignantly. "It's like something out of the 1950s."

"I can't believe Chris would talk that way about anyone," I said, always ready to defend him. "It's his jock friends."

"Well, Chris *started* those rumors," Donna said. "Lori Ann's name is *mud*."

Lori Ann, in fact, stayed out of school a whole week, supposedly home sick with the flu. When she came back, nobody bothered with her, except for a couple of guys from the basketball team who made an elaborate show of going over and talking to her. But she ignored them. Her face pale and set, Lori Ann walked to her classes all alone.

I had mixed emotions about the whole thing. I felt sorry for Lori Ann, but I still had a crush on Chris, and I didn't like it when people bad-mouthed him.

Lori Ann had been sitting alone at lunchtime, trying to ignore the smirks and whispers. Then one day somebody joined her for lunch. It was the first time anyone had bothered with her since those stories started.

I nearly flipped when I realized it was Mike Matthews sitting with Lori Ann. He sat with her the rest of the week until a couple of her old friends invited her to eat with them.

"I told you Mike was a nice guy," Donna said.

Chapter 22

I had almost forgotten about the turquoise dress Aunt Rose had bought me in Filene's last November. I was going through my closet, looking for something to wear for Awards Night, when I spotted the dress, still in its plastic bag.

"Hoo!" Aunt Rose greeted me when I came downstairs that night. "Now, at least, you *look* like something!"

That was the closest she had ever come to a compliment.

Awards Night was being held in the school cafeteria. The Jonathan Waring Committee had planned everything well—the essay awards for sophomores, the sports awards and book awards for juniors, and the various Waring scholarships for seniors.

I warned my mother and Aunt Rose that it would probably be a boring evening, particularly since the sports awards would be presented first, and the essay awards near the end of the program. I didn't think Aunt Rose would want to come with us, but she did. "I want to see how they renovated the cafeteria," she said.

The place was packed. The students sat in a reserved section near the podium. I spotted Mike Matthews, although at first I didn't recognize him dressed up in a sport jacket and tie. Chris McConnell was there, looking gorgeous in a navy blazer. Chris would be getting a sports award, along with the rest of the basketball team.

During intermission, Mike came over to talk to me. "The latest word is everyone thinks maybe the German exchange student might have won," he said. "She wrote about her host family."

"That sounds like something the judges would love," I said. "Oh, well, at least the runners-up get a plaque."

Intermission ended and we settled back for the second part of the program. I could see Aunt Rose out in the audience in her red print dress, constantly turning around to stare at everyone. I had to smile. I was kind of glad she was there.

Finally Mr. Clements, our principal, started talking about the Jonathan Waring Essay Competition. "There is only one prize awarded—a five-hundred-dollar savings bond to be used for the student's college education," Mr. Clements told the audience. "The nine runners-up will each receive a plaque. Please hold your applause until the end."

He straightened his glasses and read off the names. "The runners-up are . . . Janine Burger . . . Melissa Cohen . . . Wayne Erlich . . . Ingrid Haas . . . Donald Leung . . . Michael Matthews . . ."

Well, that was a comfort. At least Mike hadn't won first prize. Neither had the German exchange student.

"Pamela Silver . . . Craig Vieira . . ."

I was ready to stand up.

"Michele Zielinski."

All nine of the contestants had already gone up to the podium for their awards. I sat frozen in my seat.

"And now, I am pleased and honored to announce the winner of the first annual Jonathan Waring Essay Competition— Miss Kate Williams."

I couldn't believe my ears. In a daze I pushed myself from my seat and walked up to the podium as the audience burst into applause.

I distinctly heard a "Hoo!" from the section where parents and guests were seated.

Mr. Clements shook my hand. "Before I present Kate with her plaque and bond, let me say that while all the submissions were excellent, this one essay touched the hearts and minds of our judges. We think it should be shared with all of you here. So Katie, since we're ahead of our schedule tonight, I'd like to ask you to read your essay."

I was nervous enough just walking up to the podium, let alone having to read my essay out loud. But I took a deep breath as Mr. Clements handed me those familiar sheets of lined paper. He adjusted the microphone.

In a shaky voice I started to read:

> Most likely you've never even heard of her. She has never received any awards or honors. Yet she has touched the lives of everyone in this community. She has helped make her street, her neighborhood, her corner of the world, a little better, a little safer, a little more decent.
>
> She's a vanishing breed. Once upon a time, no matter where you lived, you probably knew somebody like her . . . the nosy neighbor who minded everyone's business . . . who wasn't afraid to stand up, to speak up, to get involved.
>
> There's a black family here in Pennington who will never forget that woman's courage one night many years ago. That family had moved into an all-white neighborhood, and there was a lot of racial tension and violence at the time. There was even talk of the Ku Klux Klan's burning a cross on the lawn.
>
> One of the boys in that family—who is now a judge in town—remembers that summer night very well. A menacing crowd had gathered in front of the house, yelling taunts and threats.

All of a sudden, that woman, who lived on that street, pushed her way to the front of the crowd. She grabbed the ringleader by the collar and yelled, "YOU OUGHT TO BE ASHAMED OF YOURSELVES, YOU BIG PALOOKAS. GO HOME NOW AND QUIT BOTHERING THESE PEOPLE!"

She shamed that crowd. They muttered and mumbled, but they all went home. And they did, in fact, quit bothering the people in that house. From then on, there were no more incidents.

This woman has never been afraid to rock the boat. Sometimes she's tipped it right over. She lost her first job because she complained about safety violations. She lost a job once again when she joined a union. She marched in picket lines to fight for decent wages and safe working conditions.

She never did learn to mind her own business— and it's a good thing. That's how she discovered there was a youngster being abused only a few houses away from her own. And an elderly neighbor might have died if that woman hadn't wondered why he didn't go for his usual morning stroll. She checked up on him and found the man had fallen down and broken his hip, unable to summon help.

In a world where most people say, "Look, I don't want to get involved," she's the one who writes down the license number of the hit-and-run car. She's the one who files a complaint with the Department of Social Services or the Labor Board. She's the one who witnesses a crime and calls the police.

She has stood up to the palookas and the bums and lowlifes of this world. And because of this woman and people like her, we can sleep a little better, knowing there are still a few good nosy neighbors out there, keeping an eye on things and watching out for us.

That unsung heroine is my aunt—Mrs. Rose Cronin, who opened her home and her heart to my mother and me and who taught us that justice and fairness came about because somebody, somewhere, was a nosy neighbor.

There was a hushed silence. And then the room erupted in a roar of applause.

I don't remember much about the rest of the program. After it was over, everyone gathered at the back of the cafeteria for refreshments.

My mother and Aunt Rose rushed toward me. Mom gave me a big hug. "I'm so proud of you," she kept saying over and over. There were tears in her eyes.

Aunt Rose was positively glowing. Her black eyes sparkled behind her harlequin glasses. There were two bright spots of color on her cheeks. *"I'm the one,"* she announced as she elbowed her way through the crowd. *"I'm the aunt she wrote about!"*

She grabbed me and I thought she was going to give me a hug, but instead she leaned over and whispered in my ear, "Bella Wing from the Grief Group was sitting next to me, and she almost fell off her chair when she heard the essay. Hoo, was *she* jealous!"

People kept coming over to congratulate the three of us.

There was a tap on my shoulder. I looked up to see Chris McConnell. "This calls for a celebration," he said. "A few of us are going to a party at Jack Merrick's house—would you like to go with me?"

I stared at him. It had finally happened! *Chris McConnell had noticed me!*

"I don't know," I stammered, "it's kind of late. . . ."

"Okay, then, I'll drive you home," he said easily.

I looked up into those incredibly blue eyes of his. But all I could picture was Lori Ann Baines, sitting all alone, while the kids whispered stories about her. Stories that Chris himself had spread.

"I'm going home with my family," I heard myself telling Chris. "And anyhow, I wouldn't be caught dead with you—not after the way you treated Lori Ann!"

Chris was stunned. He wasn't used to being turned down. Or put down, for that matter. He strode out of the cafeteria, his face dark with anger.

As I watched him go, it occurred to me that I had finally achieved all three of my goals . . . improving my grades, winning the essay contest, and getting Chris to ask me out.

Behind me, a familiar voice said, "The worst thing in the world is to want something badly and then to get it." I turned around and saw Mike. I hadn't realized he'd been standing there all along.

Mike held out his hand. "You done good, Katie. That was a great essay. I predict a successful writing career."

"You'd better dust off your crystal ball," I said. "I don't want to be a writer. I'm going to be a lawyer so I can help change public policy."

"Oh, a crusader. See that? You're more like your aunt Rose than you realize."

We stood there, talking and kidding around. Mike joked that the cafeteria people were trying to psych us out. "All year long, the food is horrible," he said. "But once a year on Awards Night, they come up with all this great stuff—cakes, cookies, punch. I can just hear the parents: 'I don't know why you kids always complain about the food at school—I think it's delicious.'"

My mother, who had been chatting with some people, came over to join us. Mike shook her hand.

"Congratulations, Mrs. Williams. Katie did you all proud."

The three of us talked for a while. Then Aunt Rose, who had been holding court near the refreshment table, walked over to us, carrying a plate with assorted pastries.

"I don't know why you kids always complain about the food at school," she said. "I think it's delicious."

With that, Mike and I broke up.

"Who are *you*?" she said, eyeing Mike. "I'm Aunt Rose."

"Of course you are," he said. "Who else could you be?"

"Hoo, a smart aleck." Aunt Rose likes smart alecks. She checked Mike out, head to toe. Dark, curly hair. Hazel eyes behind wire-rim glasses. White teeth. Nice mouth . . .

I blinked. Was it because he was dressed up that Mike suddenly looked different? I mean, he was actually *cute*.

"Oho, now I recognize your voice," my aunt said triumphantly. "You called Katie for a date one night and she turned you down."

"Aunt Rose," I said hurriedly, "this is my classmate, Mike Matthews."

"Matthews, Matthews," she repeated. "You're the smart boy. I remember the name. So how come Katie wouldn't go out with you?"

"Now, Rose . . ." Mom said warningly.

Aunt Rose ignored her. "You're not bad," she observed, tilting her head to get a better look at Mike. "Of course, you're no Mr. America."

"Aunt Rose!" I protested.

"But then, Katie's no Hollywood starlet *either*," she concluded.

"Rose, *please!*" My mother was turning all colors.

Aunt Rose stared at Mike, a little frown puckering her forehead. She was obviously up to something.

"Do you get good marks in history?" she said at last. "A smart boy like you?"

He shrugged modestly. "I like history."

"Well," she said, her little black eyes glittering, "if you like history, you ought to come over and listen to the oral history I did. It's all about labor unions."

"I'll bet it's very interesting," Mike said politely.

"You can come over tomorrow night and hear it. Tomorrow," she added pointedly, "is *Saturday* night."

"Fine," said Mike. "What time?"

"About seven-thirty. Then afterwards you could take Katie to the movies."

"Sounds good to me." Mike was smiling broadly. "But how do you know Katie isn't busy tomorrow night?"

"Hoo," said Aunt Rose with a wave of her hand, "believe me, she's not busy. Nobody's breaking down *her* door wanting a date."

I looked at Mom, she looked me, and all of a sudden we burst out laughing.

"Aunt Rose *means* well," Mom and I chorused.

"Most *naturally*," said Aunt Rose as she carefully wrapped some pastries in a napkin and put them into her pocketbook.

About the Author

Rona S. Zable lives with her daughter in New Bedford, Massachusetts. She is the author of numerous articles as well as two young adult novels, *Love at the Laundromat* and *An Almost Perfect Summer*, both available in Starfire paperback editions.